PEOPLE
LIKE
US

PEOPLE LIKE US

Barbara Cohen

BANTAM BOOKS
TORONTO • NEW YORK • LONDON • SYDNEY • AUCKLAND

PEOPLE LIKE US
A Bantam Book / September 1987

*The Starfire logo is a registered trademark of Bantam Books, Inc.
Registered in U.S. Patent and Trademark Office and elsewhere.*

Library of Congress Cataloging-in-Publication Data

Cohen, Barbara.
  People like us.

  Summary: Fifteen-year-old Dinah's insistence on
dating a handsome football star causes bitter dissension
in her family because the boy is not a Jew like them.
  [1. Jews—Fiction.   2. Prejudices—Fiction.
3. Family life—Fiction]   I. Title.
PZ7.C6595Pe   1987   [Fic]   √ 87-11535
ISBN 0-553-05441-4

Published simultaneously in the United States and Canada

*Bantam Books are published by Bantam Books, Inc. Its trademark, consisting
of the words "Bantam Books" and the portrayal of a rooster, is Registered in
U.S. Patent and Trademark Office and in other countries. Marca Registrada.
Bantam Books, Inc., 666 Fifth Avenue, New York, New York 10103.*

PRINTED IN THE UNITED STATES OF AMERICA

FG   0 9 8 7 6 5 4 3 2

For Becky and Andrew

PEOPLE
LIKE
US

ONE

"I think if I lick another sticky flap, I'll throw up," my brother Jonathan complained.

"Use the sponge," I suggested.

"Then the whole envelope gets wet. There're too many of them anyway." He gazed at the address on the one in his hand. "Who needs Mr. and Mrs. Milton Kasselbaum? Instead of Mr. Kasselbaum, Mrs. Kasselbaum will probably bring her Yorkshire terrier, all dressed up in its mink-trimmed coat."

"Mr. Kasselbaum was a friend of Dad's."

"Dad's been dead twelve years." He put the envelope on the ready-to-mail pile and started stuffing another. "I don't see why Mom had to invite the whole immediate world. This is just a bar mitzvah I'm having, not a coronation."

"Who do you suggest she leave out—I mean, besides the Kasselbaums?"

His eye skimmed the sheets of paper spread out in the middle of the dining-room table. "I'm really surprised Chicken Little isn't on that list. Everyone else is."

Chicken Little was the name Jonathan and I had bestowed on Elliot Chickering, our mother's boss. He was the president of a small but extremely high-class pharmaceutical company of which our mother was vice-president and sales manager. She made lots of money, which was important, because our father, who'd died of complications stemming from Vietnam injuries, had left behind nothing but his armed services life insurance policy.

"If it wasn't for Mom's job, we'd be poor," I said. "You'd have a little bar mitzvah on a Thursday morning, with some chick-peas and gefilte fish balls afterward. No party, no presents. How would you like that?"

"Oh, come on, Dinah," Jonathan said. "Gram and Gramps would see that it was done right."

"They'd try," I admitted. "But on a schoolteacher's pension they couldn't do much. Do you think we'd all be living in this house if Mom didn't have a job like the one she's got? When you make what she makes, they expect a lot in return. In this life, there's nothing for nothing."

"Dinah, shut up," Jonathan exclaimed. "You sound just like her."

I grinned. "Yeah, I know."

"You were imitating her on purpose."

I nodded.

"Well, don't. One of Mom is enough."

I punched his arm. "She's crazy about you, and you know it."

He looked at me and shrugged. "You finish, Dinah," he said. "I've got to go now. My bar mitzvah lesson is at four-thirty."

Actually, there was plenty of time, but he was always in a hurry to meet Cantor Nathanson. He wanted his bar mitzvah to be perfect. And he wanted plenty of people there to see just how perfect it was. His complaints were merely a cover for how much he cared.

"Okay." I glanced at my watch. "Gram'll be home from the shelter soon. She'll help me."

He rushed out of the room, tripping over his big feet only once. He hadn't grown into them yet. He would be tall one day, like Gramps, but that day was still years away. He had the same sweet, serious, rosy face as the little boy I used to pull behind me in a wooden wagon wherever I

2

went. Even though the difference in our ages is less than three years, I'd mothered him, and of course, so had Gram. Not that he didn't know who his mother really was. There was no confusion on that issue. In those days, Mom, Jonathan, and I spent every minute together when she was home, and when she was away she phoned each night.

But we were older now, and we were all busier. The pharmaceutical company had grown and Mom took more trips. When she *was* home, she might say, "Come on, let's go to the movies," and then Jonathan might say, "I'm going with Howard," or Gregory, or Tommy, or whoever. Yet that didn't stop him from griping about her absences. He was like a first-grader who wants his mother waiting to serve him milk and cookies when he gets off the school bus, even though two minutes later he runs out to play and doesn't come back into the house until six o'clock.

I picked up one of the invitations and read it over for the nine-millionth time.

> *Twenty-nine Silver Lane*
> *Lenape, New Jersey 07582*

My son, Jonathan, will be called to the Torah as a Bar Mitzvah on Saturday, April fourth, nineteen hundred and eighty-seven, at nine o'clock in the morning at Temple Shalom, Normandy Avenue, Lenape, New Jersey.

I invite you to worship with us on this joyous occasion and join us afterward for kiddush. A luncheon reception will follow at Clover Lake Country Club.

> *Ellen Adler*

The favor of a reply is requested.

The invitations were going out in Mother's name. She was making the party. She was in charge of this event. She could invite who she wanted.

3

Except for the ticking of the huge grandfather clock in the front hall, the house was silent. I continued stuffing and sealing envelopes. It was a mindless task; I didn't have to think about it. I could think about Geoffrey Ruggles instead.

He'd turned up in art class that morning, the first day of the spring semester. I'd been concentrating so hard on a still life with a bunch of purple heather which I was doing in pastels that I didn't hear him come in. But when I looked up, there he was in the front of the room, showing Mr. Wolleck a schedule card. Mr. Wolleck said something, and then Geoff took a seat. I lowered my head to my work, but with sidelong glances I was still looking at him.

There were at least two reasons for those glances. First, he was a hunk. And second, I was curious. What was Lenape High's star quarterback doing in an art class? Football players didn't draw or paint. He must have had a hole in his schedule and this was the only thing his guidance counselor could think of to fill it up.

I glanced at Claire Kincaid. No surprise there. She was also staring at Geoff. She turned, caught my eye, and grinned. I grinned, too. Claire had a boyfriend, a very nice one. But she could still look. You'd have to be dead not to look at Geoff Ruggles.

Afterward, walking to our sixth-period classes, I teased Claire. "I'm going to tell Charlie you were drooling over Geoff Ruggles."

"Weren't you?" she retorted.

"I'm unattached," I replied self-righteously.

"If Charlie can drool over Fran Mangarelli, I guess I can drool over Geoff Ruggles." She laughed a little. "In both cases, it means about as much as drooling over a rock star."

I nodded. Fran and Geoff were equally beyond the reach of the likes of us. "You know, it's funny," I said. "Neither Fran nor Geoff would even recognize us if we loomed up in front of them as big as elephants, but we know all about them."

"That's what I mean," Claire said. "You know all about

4

movie actors, but would any one of Hollywood's rich and famous know all about you? In this school, Geoff and Fran are celebrities."

"Hey, wait up!" A voice like a siren cut through the noise of the crowd. We stopped and turned. It was Charlie, rushing to catch up with us. We moved to the side of the corridor to avoid being knocked over. In a moment, Charlie reached us. We began walking again—Claire between Charlie and me, holding his hand.

"Geoff Ruggles showed up in our art class today," I informed him. "Isn't that funny?"

"I guess if I can take chorus, Geoff Ruggles can take art," Charlie said.

Both Claire and I refrained from mentioning that Charlie Hoagland was not Geoff Ruggles. An occasional workout at the Y was the extent of Charlie's athletic activity. But that was okay. His spare time was spent working at the Lenape Animal Hospital. He already knew he wanted to be a veterinarian. In spite of the fact that Charlie's whisper sounded like another person's shout, he was just about the gentlest, nicest guy I knew. I would have been happy to be the girlfriend of someone like Charlie. Not of Charlie, of course. Charlie was Claire's boyfriend.

"Listen, Dinah," Charlie boomed, "this is your big chance. Geoff is free. Go after him."

"Yeah, yeah." I laughed, but I wasn't really amused. To tell the truth, I had no idea of how to "go after" a boy, and Charlie and Claire both knew it. In sixth grade, Claire and I had scorned the girls who flirted with guys. We told each other they were disgusting. In seventh grade, we were a little jealous. In eighth grade, we regarded the popular kids—which meant the kids who dated—with avid interest. We were not among them. By the time we got to ninth grade, we were mooning over this guy and that guy, meanwhile bemoaning the fact that not one of them was interested in us.

Then, over the summer, something happened to Claire. She came together somehow. Not me. I was still tall and skinny and flat-chested, with arms and legs too long for my torso, and unimpressive light brown hair that looked like everyone else's. Between freshman and sophomore years Claire lost her baby fat and turned up in the fall with a perfectly proportioned figure, a whole new wardrobe, and the self-confidence born of attracting the interest of a division head at the Y camp where she'd been working. And then Charlie appeared. The division head, who lived in East Brunswick anyway, was forgotten. Charlie was now my friend, too. But things weren't the same between Claire and me. How could they be?

"Why not go after Geoff?" Claire asked. "Why not try?" She constantly urged me on, like a cheerleader, as if my dateless state, like being skinny, could be overcome if I only put my mind to it. It was one of the things about her that annoyed me now.

"No matter how gorgeous he is, my grandmother would kill me if I went out with a boy who wasn't Jewish," I said. "Mom and Gramps too, maybe." Since the chances of my being asked out by the likes of Geoff Ruggles were about one in a trillion, the problem wasn't going to come up. But at least by raising that issue, I could get Charlie and Claire to shut up.

Only they didn't. Anyway, Claire didn't. "Oh, I can't believe that," she said. "Your grandmother's neat. She never struck me as narrow-minded. You don't really believe she'd object to a simple little date with Lenape's own superstar?"

"My grandmother isn't narrow-minded," I replied. She'd demonstrated against the Vietnam War, for civil rights, and against nuclear arms. She often said that if she were twenty years younger, she'd join the Peace Corps. "But her grand-daughter going out with a non-Jew—that's different."

"Your grandmother spends hours each week at the JINS shelter," Claire said. The letters stood for Juveniles In Need of Supervision.

"Yeah, I know. And even though my grandfather doesn't march or volunteer, he says he's done his bit for the human

6

race by spending forty years working in public schools. Now he writes checks. Honestly, Claire," I said, "after all this time that we've been friends, I still can't explain it to you. The business of Jews dating gentiles is something else, that's all. My grandparents aren't so open-minded on that issue." We'd reached the end of the corridor and had to separate, I to turn right for Algebra II, Charlie and Claire to disappear in the opposite direction. I waved and hurried off.

Now, hours later, I sat in my dining room stuffing envelopes, listening to the radio, and dreaming that in art class Geoff Ruggles came up to me and said, "Dinah, I've noticed your beautiful soul. Will you come to the Student Council Dance with me?" It was a good dream, because it was perfectly safe. It could never happen. If I dreamed about someone more likely, I'd have to get upset when the dream showed no signs of coming true.

I heard the back door slam and the noise of bundles being dumped on the counter. Gram was home. I rose and entered the kitchen. "Oh, darling," she said when she saw me, "help me bring in the rest of the groceries. Where's Jonathan? He can help, too."

"He had a bar mitzvah lesson with Cantor Nathanson this afternoon. He rode his bike over." In addition to attending Hebrew school two afternoons a week, kids at Temple Shalom who were approaching bar or bat mitzvah had to prepare their special part of the Sabbath service with the cantor.

"Oh, that's right. I'd forgotten," Gram said. "Between the bar mitzvah, and his clarinet, and the Scouts, he has so much going on these days, it's hard to keep it all straight."

"Yeah," I agreed. "It's a good thing Mom made that calendar for him, so he doesn't forget."

"Boy, I'm glad someone around here is organized." She headed back toward the garage. I followed.

The car trunk was open and still packed full of grocery bags. "Who's coming for dinner?" I asked. "The entire graduating class at West Point?"

7

"You know your mother'll be here tomorrow."

"She doesn't eat much." Mom and I looked something alike. Like me, she didn't have much in the way of extra flesh on her bones. But while you'd call me skinny, you'd call her slender. Furthermore, she was beautiful. However, she had reached the age at which she had to watch herself in order to maintain her figure.

"I decided to buy a few special things she really likes," Gram said. "And that you like, too." She'd given up on Mom. Now she was trying to fatten me up.

Other than the menu, the following evening was a regular Friday night. Mom and Gram lit the Sabbath candles. Gramps chanted the blessing over the wine. Each of us took a sip from the elaborately engraved silver kiddush cup. Jonathan recited the blessing over the bread. He cut five slices from the twisted challah loaf and passed them out to each of us. When we finished eating, Gramps led the blessing after meals and some other songs, too—the special Sabbath songs we'd been singing every Friday night for as long as I could remember.

My mother leaned back in her chair with a sigh. "It's so good to be home," she said. "It's the best thing."

"Then don't go away again," Jonathan said.

"Well, I won't," she said. "Not right away."

"Yeah, yeah," Jonathan said. It was a phrase we both used. We'd picked it up from Gram.

"I mean it," she said. "I don't have another trip scheduled until early March."

"Where are you going then?" Jonathan asked.

"Sydney."

"Sydney, Australia?"

She nodded. "That's the only Sydney I've ever heard of. I wonder who he was, that Sydney. Was he Mr. Something Sydney, or Mr. Sydney Something?"

But Jonathan didn't smile. He left the table and went up to his room. In a few moments we could hear the sorrowful wailing of his clarinet as he played "Blues in the Night."

Gram and Gramps went to synagogue. Mom said she was too tired; she'd go in the morning with Jonathan. They'd been invited to Tommy Eichel's bar mitzvah. Jonathan attended a bar or bat mitzvah at least every other weekend. Sometimes Mom and even Gram and Gramps were invited, too.

It had been the same with me when I was thirteen. I hadn't minded the actual bar mitzvahs at services Saturday mornings, but the receptions were silly. At least half of the thirteen-year-olds in this world don't really enjoy parties where the main activities are conversation and dancing. Now that I was almost sixteen, I might have fun at such an event. But since my friends and I were all past the bar mitzvah stage, I didn't get invited to them anymore. Well, maybe it was just as well. I hadn't really changed much since I was thirteen. No one had asked me to dance then; no one would ask me now.

Mom and I cleaned up. She rinsed the dishes; I loaded them in the dishwasher. "Listen," she said, "what's eating Jonathan? Why's he mad at me?"

I told her the truth. "He's afraid you won't show up at his bar mitzvah. He's been worrying about that for days, and then when you said Sydney in March, it was easy for him to imagine your not making it back by April fourth."

"It's his nature to worry," Mom said. "If he hasn't got any real problems, he makes a few up."

"Australia's awfully far away."

She nodded. "Okay. I'll talk to him." She paused for a moment and looked at me. "What about you, Dinah?"

"What about me? I'm not mad at you."

"No, I mean how are you?"

"Fine. Haven't had a cold all winter."

"That's not what I'm talking about."

"I'm good, Mom. You know about my painting of the gazebo in Clover Lake Park." It took a second-place ribbon in the Lenape Valley Art Association's winter show.

"I was thrilled out of my mind when you told me." She nibbled at a little piece of the veal Gramps had left untouched on his plate. "As soon as I hung up with you, I had to tell somebody, so I called Elliot Chickering and told him."

"That show's not just for kids," I said. "A whole bunch of grown-ups exhibit, too. Even some people who sell their work."

"Did Gram exhibit in the craft section?"

"No. The tablecloth still isn't finished. She'll enter it next year. It'll probably take her that long to get it done." Gram was always fussing with needlepoint, embroidery, anything that required a good eye and good hands. Though she had never painted, I was convinced that whatever artistic talent I had, I'd inherited from her.

"That tablecloth is her chef d'oeuvre," Mom said. "Her masterpiece. We'll never be able to use it. We'll have to give it to an art museum."

Gram had been working on the cloth, which she'd designed herself, for months. She'd completed the embroidering of a shimmering greenish-blue vase. Now she was stitching the enormous bouquet that grew out of it, containing maybe a hundred different blossoms, each one depicted with painstaking accuracy. She copied them from pictures in a little book she kept in her work basket, which, in addition to full color plates, contained brief passages describing each blossom's significance in the language of flowers. As she undertook a new bloom, she'd tell us what it meant. Right now she was working on an almond blossom. That, she claimed, symbolized hope.

Mother picked up another plate and held it under the running water. "What else?"

"What do you mean, what else?"

"What else about your life?" She was like Gramps wandering into the TV room during the last five minutes of a mystery movie and asking, "What's happening?"

"There is nothing else," I said.

"Are you bringing someone to Jonathan's bar mitzvah?"

"What do you mean?"

"You know what I mean. A date. Someone to dance with."

"I'll dance with Uncle Melvin."

"You'd have more fun if you'd bring a date."

I jammed three knives, points down, into the silverware basket. "Mother, I have no one to ask. You know I have no one to ask."

She handed me a bunch of spoons. "I don't know anything of the sort. You go to Hebrew high school Sunday mornings. Why can't you ask one of those boys?"

"Oh, Mother." What was the use of explaining? None of those boys were any more interested in me than they had been two and a half years ago, when we were going through our own bar and bat mitzvahs. There were only a handful of them anyway. Lenape, New Jersey, was not exactly Brooklyn, New York. It wasn't loaded with Jews.

"What about Paul Levy?" she suggested. "He seems like a nice guy."

"He's not."

"When I play bridge at his parents' house—"

"He may seem nice to you. He does not seem nice to me." She must have forgotten what had happened between me and Paul in eighth grade. Or maybe I'd never even told her.

"Well, you think about it," she said. "I know you'll have more fun if you bring someone."

"Look, Mother," I snapped, "I'm not like you. I'm not popular. I'm not beautiful. Boys are not interested in me. Okay? So I don't want to hear any more about it."

"What do you mean, you're not beautiful? You're stunning. Most girls would give their souls for your figure."

"For my flat chest? Are you crazy?"

"You have a perfect figure for clothes. You look good in whatever you put on."

I laughed grimly. "If it's true, you're the only one who's noticed."

She slapped a big serving fork down on the counter in front of me. "How do you know?"

"I know, that's all."

"You're selling yourself short, Dinah. I don't like it."

"Oh, Mother!" I exclaimed yet again. She saw me through her eyes, a mother's eyes. And she saw me as a reflection of herself. She always had some guy or other hanging around. If she hadn't married again, it wasn't for lack of opportunity. She would never understand that I was nothing like her at all.

"Oh, Dinah," she echoed.

"Listen," I said, "I'll have a good time at Jonathan's bar mitzvah. I'll have a wonderful time. I promise. Okay? Can we drop the subject now?"

"Yes," she said. And then she added in a low voice, "For the time being." I heard. And she meant me to hear. The conversation wasn't over.

TWO

At least once every evening for the week she was home, Mom bugged me about asking someone to Jonathan's party. I was glad when she flew up to Boston for a couple of days.

Jonathan carried her bag out to the car. She was driving herself to the airport. "You told us you weren't going away again until March," he said.

"I meant no *major* trips until March," Mom replied. "Boston's so close, it doesn't count." She opened the back door and Jonathan tossed the carryall on the floor.

"It counts to me," he said.

"For heaven's sake, Jonathan," Mother protested, "if you were home two evenings in the last week, it was a lot, and those two evenings you certainly didn't spend with me." She turned to me with a lift of her brow. "It's interesting who hands out the guilt around here, isn't it? Not the grandparents. Not the mother. The son!" She put her arm around Jonathan. "I swear to you . . . I swear to you on a stack of Bibles a mile high that I will be at your bar mitzvah. Not only that, I will take off from work the two days preceding to help you get ready."

"Help me get ready?" Even Jonathan had to smile at that notion. "What can you do?"

13

"I don't know. Iron your shirt? Pick your suit up from the tailor? Listen to your speech? Wipe the nervous sweat from your brow? We'll think of something." She hugged him, kissed me, climbed into the car, turned on the ignition, waved, and drove off.

We went back in the house to finish breakfast. I left again a few minutes later to catch the bus. My classes began at eight o'clock. Jonathan didn't have to be at the middle school until eight-thirty.

Art class came right after lunch. I looked forward to it all morning. Not that I minded most of my other classes. Except for history, with Mr. Nydecker, who should have been crowned king of the bores, they were all right. But art I loved. Art absorbed all of me.

I was gazing at my still life when Mr. Wolleck stopped at my easel. "Well, what do you think?" I asked. "Do you think it's done?" For me, that was the hardest thing—knowing when to stop tinkering, knowing the moment at which more changes would make it worse instead of better. That was why Mr. Wolleck had urged me to do this piece in pastels. It was harder to make changes in pastels than it was in some other media, and he thought it was time for me to try to stop second-guessing myself so much.

"Yes," he said, "I think it's done."

"Do you think the branch is okay? Do you think I got the bark right—all those different browns?"

"I think it's quite wonderful, Dinah." He handed me a can of fixative. "Spray it," he ordered.

"You're sure?"

"You're the one who has to be sure," he said. "But think of the still life you did in the fall. Look at the progress this one represents."

"Thanks to you," I said.

His smile lit his eyes. "It's very nice of you to say that, Dinah. But you have a lot of talent."

"I had talent last year, too. But I didn't accomplish in last year's art class what I've accomplished this year." First-

14

year art had been structured. Miss Wantrobski taught lessons built around different media and forms. Art II with Mr. Wolleck was more like a studio, in which we each worked on our own projects.

"You needed last year's foundation to build on this year," he said.

I nodded. I knew what he was saying was true.

"I'm confident you'll go even further with your next still life," he added. "But on this one, it's time to stop. You don't want to tire of it. You need a change of pace."

I nodded again. "I was thinking of trying a charcoal next," I said. "A drawing of my brother, to give to my mother for her birthday."

"Good idea. Bring in a photograph." His finger tapped a corner of the still life. "Don't put this in your portfolio just yet. Hang it up on the bulletin board. We're going to take a period next week and critique some things. I'd like this to be among them. It'll be helpful to the others to realize that someone in the class can work on this level."

"Thanks." My grin must have stretched across my whole face. I knew he liked my work; he'd given me A's all year. But this was the first time he'd told me I had talent, and he wasn't a person who threw praise around like fingerpaint.

His smile as he moved off down the aisle was as broad as mine. I picked up the spray can and went to work. It was too bad for me that Mr. Wolleck was bald, a grandfather, and extremely attached to his very nice wife. I knew what to do to attract the admiration of the Mr. Wollecks of this world. If they were over forty, they liked me a lot. All of Gramps's friends were just crazy about me.

When the spray dried, I carried the pastel to the bulletin board, which covered the whole side wall of the room. I studied the board for a while, looking for the best spot in which to hang it. I tacked it up, decided the red and black collage next to it overwhelmed it, took it down, and tacked it up again below a watercolor. Standing back to evaluate the effect, I judged myself satisfied. I turned to go back to my seat.

Standing scarcely two feet behind me, a boy was gazing thoughtfully at my picture. "Pretty good," he said. "Pretty darn good." It was Geoff Ruggles.

"Pretty good!" I retorted. "Pretty good! It's excellent!"

He grinned. "Okay. I accept that. Excellent. You want to help?"

"Help? Help do what?"

"Decorate for the Student Council Dance. We could use you."

I wasn't going to the dance. That was the thought which shot through my brain the minute he said the word. Why should I knock myself out making decorations for it? "People think if you do one kind of art, you do all kinds," I returned stiffly. "Actually, I'm a painter. I'm really not very good at paper chains and all that artsy-craftsy stuff. The committee wouldn't want me."

"The committee wants you."

"How can you be so sure?"

He laughed. "I'm the chairman."

"You?"

He wasn't smiling anymore. "You sound like you don't believe me."

"I know you're not lying. . . ."

"Then what's the problem?"

I shook my head. "You're—you're a football player."

"So . . . ?"

I hesitated. Whatever I might say next would sound even dumber than what I'd said already. It seemed best at that point just to keep my mouth shut.

"Are you trying to say that quarterbacks can't decorate gyms?"

"It surprises me, that's all," I said. "Art class, decorating committee—it just surprises me."

"You're kind of narrow-minded, aren't you?" He didn't sound angry, merely curious. "Painters don't make dance decorations; football players don't make dance decorations. We keep this up and the only decorations for that dance will be the basketball lines on the floor."

16

"You don't even know me," I retorted, stung. "The last thing I am is narrow-minded. It's just that . . . oh, never mind." I turned away, anxious to retreat to the safety of my chair and my easel.

"I do know you," he said. "Your name is Dinah."

Startled, I paused and turned toward him again. "How did you know that?" And then I realized. "Of course. My signature, on the still life."

He nodded. "Will you help?" He turned the full force of his Robert Redford smile on me.

Boy, he was sure of himself. He thought all he had to do was flash his phony grin and any girl would forget any mean thing he'd said. Narrow-minded. He'd called me narrow-minded. Well, he started in on the wrong one when he started in on me. "I said no," I replied in careful, clipped tones. I wanted to be sure he understood. "I meant no." Without another word, I returned to my seat.

But I realized that now I was blushing. I covered my face with my hands and breathed deeply. I knew I should get up, find some paper, some charcoal, start sketching. But I couldn't. My arms and legs were trembling.

I sighed with relief when I heard the bell ring. It was the first time in my life I was glad art class was over. Claire, two aisles closer to the door, waited for me. Putting my hand on her arm, I whispered, "Hold back a minute." Once I made sure that Geoff had left the classroom, I released her. "Okay. Now we can go."

"What's the matter with you?" Claire asked. "You're acting crazy." She peered at me. "You look crazy, too."

"I just had a conversation with Geoff Ruggles."

"I know!" she exclaimed. "I saw. What were you talking about?"

"Oh, nothing," I said. "Nothing important. He asked me to join the committee that's decorating for the Student Council Dance. I told him no, of course."

"You told him no, of course!" She grabbed my shoulder and shook me. "You really are crazy."

"Making chains out of colored construction paper is

even more boring than listening to Mr. Nydecker. Anyway, I'm not going to the dance. Why should I decorate for it?" I started down the hall.

Claire matched her stride to mine. My legs were about six inches longer than hers, and she had to stretch them to keep up. "But he asked you to. Geoff Ruggles asked you to. Is he on the committee?"

"He's the chairman," I admitted.

"You would have seen him every day, after school. You would have worked with him. Who knows what might have happened?"

"Nothing would have happened." I felt a great wave of anger wash over me. "Nothing at all. I would have slaved away on decorations, he wouldn't have spoken to me except to give me orders, and then I wouldn't even have gone to the dance. Who needs it? Especially now that I'm so busy with Jonathan's bar mitzvah and all." That was a lie. Except for buying a dress, I didn't have a single responsibility regarding Jonathan's bar mitzvah. The work was all his.

"Dinah . . ." She stopped walking.

"Yes?" I stopped walking, too.

"Don't you have a crush on Geoff Ruggles?"

"Not anymore."

"I think you behaved like a world-class idiot."

"Maybe I am a world-class idiot. Look, don't mention it again. And don't talk about it to Charlie."

"I won't."

I didn't really believe her. I was almost sorry I'd told her. But because she'd seen Geoff talking to me I had to tell her something.

"Listen," she said, "it isn't too late. Tell him you changed your mind. Tell him you'd be glad to help."

I shook my head.

Her eyes narrowed as she stared at me. "You know what I think, Dinah? I think you're scared. I think you're scared of liking a real boy. You just said you don't have a crush on Geoff anymore. That's because he talked to you. He stepped out of his movie magazine and talked to you.

18

So now you can't like him anymore. Because he's real, and you're afraid he might not like you back."

"Listen, Claire," I snapped, "I really don't need to be psychoanalyzed. Not by you."

"Are you mad at me? Don't be mad at me, Dinah."

"I'm not mad at you." Because I had held her back leaving the classroom, Charlie was ahead of us instead of behind us. I could see him waiting by the lockers where we usually connected following art class. We had to pass the door to the library first. "Look," I said, "I'm going in here. I have to drop off a book. I'll speak to you tonight."

"You're mad at me."

"I'm not mad at you." I waved briefly and scuttled through the library door. I wasn't mad at her. But I was annoyed, more at myself than at her. She was right. Claire didn't have to tell me I'd behaved like an idiot. I knew it. I knew I'd spoken to Geoff Ruggles as if I were some sort of stuck-up snob. And the business about being afraid of a real boy—well, maybe there was some truth in that, too. In eighth grade I'd asked Paul Levy to the Sadie Hawkins Dance. Claire and some of the other girls had talked me into it. They had it on good authority that he liked me. Although I'd never seen any evidence to support such a claim, I allowed myself to be persuaded. They'd been misinformed. He turned me down flat. No reason, no hemming and hawing, just an amazed "No," as if my even asking him suggested I was out of my mind. Since then, I'd confined my risk-taking to paper and canvas. Any boy I ever got involved with would have to show me that he liked me—a lot. He'd have to ask me first.

The thing to do, I told myself, was just to forget that Geoff had spoken to me. Forget about it altogether. Forget it had ever happened. The other thing to do was to stop dreaming about him. Find someone else to dream about. Preferably someone there wasn't the remotest chance of meeting in the flesh.

I lectured myself in some such fashion for the rest of the afternoon. By the time I got home, I felt better enough to sit with Jonathan and listen to him practice his *haftarah*. He sounded wonderful. He knew it all. He knew it so well that now the cantor was working with him on other parts of the Sabbath service. He was going to be a star.

The phone rang. "I'll get it," I said to Jonathan. "Keep singing!" I ran into the kitchen and picked up the receiver.

"Dinah?"

I recognized the whine in her voice. "Yes, Erna." I wondered if she would recognize the sigh in mine.

If she did, she paid no attention. "Can I come over? I need some help with my algebra."

"Now is not a good time, Erna. I'm helping Jonathan with his *haftarah* now."

"In half an hour?"

"I'll be working with Jonathan a lot longer than half an hour." Jonathan knew his *haftarah* as well as he knew his own name, but I was trying to discourage Erna. In my present mood I didn't really have the strength to deal with her.

But she was not easily discouraged. "After supper, then," she said.

"I'm going out after supper."

"You have to help me, Dinah. If you don't help me, I'll fail algebra."

"Oh, all right." Who had died and left me Erna? But I knew how persistent she was. If I didn't give in today, I'd have to help her tomorrow. You couldn't actually escape Erna. "Come on over. But I can only give you half an hour. When Gram comes home, I have to help her with supper." I always tried to make Erna think I was so busy I scarcely had time to take a bath.

She was at the door in two minutes. She lived only half a block away, but still, she must have run all the way. With her long, dirty brown hair flying in ten directions and her soiled shirttail hanging out from beneath her parka, she looked as if she were about to fall apart. "I'm here," she said breathlessly.

"Yes, so I see. Come on in." We sat at the dining-room

20

table. Jonathan mumbled a greeting and disappeared upstairs. He had even less patience for Erna than I had.

"You think I could eat supper here?" she asked. "Dad's working late and Mom had to take Barry to some hospital in New York for special tests. They're staying overnight. I hate eating alone, and I have to do it all the time. It's miserable."

"I don't know, Erna. You'll have to ask Gram." But I knew Gram would say yes. Gram felt sorry for Erna. Her brother Barry, who'd been born with a heart defect, seemed to take all her mother's time and energy, and work seemed to take all her father's. According to Erna, neither of them had anything left over for her. I suppose I should have felt sorry, but Erna felt so sorry for herself that no one else needed to. It was hard to blame her parents for preferring Barry, who was intelligent, handsome, and unfailingly good-natured in spite of his medical problems. Erna wasn't dumb, but she sure acted it, and she always looked like a rag doll a thoughtless child had left out in the rain. That didn't seem to bother Gram. She couldn't resist an unhappy kid any more than Charlie Hoagland could resist a bedraggled puppy.

I opened the algebra book. "What's the problem?" I asked.

"Page two hundred thirteen. They're all problems." She rested her chin in one hand, and with the other she twisted, untwisted, and retwisted a lock of her hair. "I can't do any of them. I don't understand quadratic equations and I never will. It's because of Mrs. Auslander. She doesn't explain anything."

"It's all right, Erna," I soothed. "We'll get to the bottom of it." I asked her some questions about the first problem on the page, trying to lead her to the solution step-by-step. She answered most of them correctly. Math wasn't really beyond Erna. She could have grasped the material herself if she'd studied it for a while. She came over not because she needed help with her homework, but because she was lonesome.

"You're wonderful," she announced when we were done. "You're absolutely wonderful."

"Come off it, Erna."

"You're a true friend, Dinah."

She acted as if I were more than a friend. She was a year younger than I, and she treated me like an older sister. If that's how she thought of me, she was in a lot of trouble. When she'd first moved to our street, we'd both been in the middle school, she in fifth grade and I in sixth. She'd tried to sit next to me on the bus. I explained to her that I saved the seat for Claire. Then she started moving next to me if she saw that Claire didn't get on at her stop. Since Claire always called to let me know if she was going to be absent, I learned to squeeze in with Josie and Brenda on those days. So Erna ended up sitting alone, except when the bus was so crowded there was no other seat. Then the girl who had to share with her sat with her feet in the aisle and her back to Erna.

Of course, it was different now that we were in high school. But not all that different. A person occupying the space next to Erna no longer felt obliged to sit sideways. However, like most high schools, Lenape was full of cliques. Mine wasn't the important crowd. It wasn't the popular crowd. Nevertheless, I fit in with Claire and Josie and Brenda. I fit in someplace. Erna Ammerman didn't seem to fit in anywhere. Still, out of twelve hundred kids, I figured there had to be one she could hang out with.

"Listen, Erna," I said, looking her right in the eye, "I think you ought to find some friends in your grade. It would be better for you to sort of broaden your horizons." It wasn't a terribly subtle remark. But I'd decided that, for Erna's sake as well as my own, it was necessary to be blunt.

"I should, but it's hard. The kids in our school are such snobs." She always twisted the same piece of hair, and now she was working on it so vigorously I was surprised it didn't fall out. "I know you don't have a lot of time for me. I know Claire's your best friend. It would be nice to be one person's favorite. Just one person."

"Look, Erna, Mom and Gram and Gramps love me, but they love Jonathan just as much. Claire loves me, but she loves Charlie more nowadays. Brenda and Josie love me, but they love each other better. Still, I'm surviving, even though I'm not anyone's favorite, either. Except maybe Mr. Wolleck's." However, I did kind of understand what Erna was talking about. It *would* be wonderful to have someone love you best. "Stay for dinner," I suggested. "I know it'll be all right with Gram."

It was, of course. Gram was pleased to have her and kept offering her seconds and even thirds. It was Gram's opinion that Erna needed fattening up. But it wasn't such a pleasant meal for me. I couldn't stand Erna's adoration. It was an embarrassment to me.

I really was going out after dinner. Gramps was driving me to the library to do some research on my history term paper. I was writing about congressional attitudes toward immigration from 1882, the year the first federal law restricting immigration was passed, up until the present. It sounds boring, but it wasn't. Working on it was a lot more interesting than listening to Mr. Nydecker.

"I'll come with you," Erna said. "I can sit and read while you're studying. I won't bother you."

I'd had enough for one day. I wasn't interested in earning a halo. "Don't you have some other homework besides the algebra?"

"A little Spanish."

"You better go home and do it. Gramps will drop you on our way to the library."

"I have an idea." She sounded as if she'd just invented the wheel. "I'll run into my house, pick up my Spanish book, and take it to the library. Then you can help me with it there."

"Erna, I never studied Spanish. I know nothing about it. Not one single word. I take French, remember?"

"They must be something alike."

I resorted to direct measures. "To get this kind of

research done, I absolutely must be alone. I think it's time for you to go home."

Gram shot me a questioning glance, which I pretended to ignore. "You can stay here and help me clean up," she suggested.

"No, that's all right," Erna said, in a tone she might have used to announce she was being forced to give up ice cream for life. "I'll just go on home. You don't need to drop me, Mr. Horowitz. I can walk."

"It's dark, Erna," Gramps said. "I'll drop you."

"No, really, it's all right. I don't want to put you out."

"I'll drop you."

She ceased protesting. Gramps waited in front of her house until he saw a light go on in the front hall. "Okay," he said, pulling the car away from the curb. "She got in all right. She's the kind of person who could suffer a major disaster between the car and the front door."

"Yeah," I agreed. "It's no fun being around her. But Gram gets annoyed if I'm anything less than perfectly lovely to her."

"Gram feels sorry for her."

"Yeah, she and Gram connect, all right. So let Gram help her with her algebra."

Gramps laughed, and said no more. I think, so far as Erna was concerned, Gramps was more on my side than he was on Gram's.

In the library, I gathered together half a dozen books that I needed, carried them to a work table, and sat down. From my purse I removed an unopened package of three-by-five file cards and two fine felt-tipped pens, one black and one red. The red ink was for bibliographical information, the black ink for notes. When I had all my materials arranged around me in the way that I liked, I began working. But one book leads to another, and after a while, I had to get up again and check the card catalog in order to find out if the library owned the volumes to which some of my sources were referring.

I pulled out a catalog drawer and rested it on the shelf.

A couple of boys walked by, headed for the circulation desk. I looked up to see who they were, and felt my cheeks turn hot. The two boys in the whole world whom I least wanted to meet—for more or less opposite reasons. One was Paul Levy. The other was Geoff Ruggles. I thought I'd talked myself out of him. Was I going to blush furiously every time I laid eyes on him? That would be ridiculous, since I had to see him five days a week in art class.

He glanced in my direction. For a moment, our eyes held. Then he turned away and moved on. But I had looked in his face long enough to be startled by his expression. It reminded me a little of one I often saw Erna wear when her feelings had been hurt, which happened at least nine times a day. Geoff's countenance contained no element of self-pity, but the corners of his mouth were turned down and his usually sparkling eyes held a kind of mournfulness. A surprising idea crossed my mind. Maybe I'd done to Geoff Ruggles what I'd done so often to Erna. Maybe I had hurt his feelings. Maybe I had made him feel bad. I wouldn't have thought it possible.

I abandoned the catalog drawer and hurried toward the circulation desk. I wished with all my heart that I was a witch and could make Paul Levy disappear. But since I couldn't, I'd have to say what I had to say in front of him, too. They were waiting in line to check out. I marched myself right between them.

"Hey," Paul exclaimed, "what's the big idea? I was here first; get behind me." He didn't even use my name. Of course, he knew it. We'd been in the same Hebrew school class for eight years.

"Don't worry, Paul, I'm not checking out a book. I just want to talk to Geoff." My stomach was turning over inside of me, but I was managing to maintain a calm exterior. It was fortunate I'd acted on my impulse. If I'd thought about it for two seconds, I'd probably have walked out of the library through a back door.

Geoff turned. His lifted brows formed a question mark,

25

but he didn't say anything. Clearly, the ball was in my court, and he wasn't climbing over any nets to get it.

"Look, Geoff, I'm sorry about this morning." My words rushed out of my mouth, stepping on each other's tails. "I acted like an idiot. I don't know what got into me. I'd be very happy to serve on the decorating committee. I still don't think I'll be very good at it, but I'd like to help, if you still want me."

His face broke out in his broad, irresistible grin. "If we still want you? Of course we want you. Paper chains are just what we're trying to get away from. We're desperate for an artist's imagination."

I could recognize a compliment when I heard it. "Thanks," I murmured.

"We're meeting after school tomorrow in Mr. Wolleck's room."

"I'll be there."

We stood for a moment, a sudden awkwardness between us. I spoke first. "Okay, then. I better get back to my history paper. See you tomorrow."

He lifted his hand in half a wave. I returned to the card catalog, still shaking inside, but satisfied. I had redeemed myself. I no longer felt like either a fool or a meanie.

The library did have one of the books I wanted. While I was searching the nine hundred shelves to see if it was in, Geoff reappeared. "Here you are, Dinah," he said. "Lucky you said history paper, or I'd never have found you."

Now it was my turn to look at him with a question on my face.

"Can I give you a lift home?" he asked. "My car looks like Rent-A-Wreck, but it's safe."

I could call Gramps. I could tell him he didn't have to pick me up. Glancing at my watch, I saw that it was a quarter to nine. He must have already left the house.

"Thanks, Geoff," I said. "That's really nice of you. But my grandfather is coming for me. He's probably on his way now."

"Another time, then."

"Yes."

"So long, Dinah."

"So long, Geoff."

For a moment after he had gone, I stood in the aisle between the stacks of shelves, clutching *Immigration and the American Experience* to my breast like a baby. Another time, he'd said. Another time. It would be better another time. Paul Levy wouldn't be with him.

THREE

The next day, in art class, Geoff gave me a big hello. I gave him a big hello back. By working hard on Jonathan's portrait, I managed not to glance in his direction any more than eight or nine times. He was hunched over his easel, too, concentrating.

"I saw that," Claire said in the hall afterward.

"Saw what?"

"Saw Geoff speak to you when you walked by him."

"Don't make anything of it, Claire." I'd resolved not to hope. If you don't hope, you can't be disappointed. Dreams are different. They're okay, so long as you know the difference between them and reality. But now that I was actually acquainted with Geoff, dreams were hopes, so I tried to make myself ditch them, too.

"Something must have happened," Claire said.

"I met him in the library last night and I apologized. So now I'm on the decorating committee."

"And you didn't tell me? You didn't call me last night. You didn't mention it on the bus this morning. You let a whole art period go by without saying a word." She struck her chest with her open palm. "Dinah, this is me, Claire, your buddy."

"There was nothing to tell."

"Well, I saw the way he said hello to you. And I saw the way you said hello to him. There's something to tell, all right."

"No, there isn't," I replied firmly. "If there were, you'd be the first to know."

"When does that committee meet?"

"This afternoon," I admitted.

"I'm calling you tonight. I'm not waiting for you to call me."

"I'll have nothing to report," I assured her. "Nothing at all."

I only half believed that. Hope had turned into an elflike creature who, in spite of my resolve to kill her, kept popping up in my brain. I really had to scream at her to shut her up.

That I hadn't succeeded was proved by the way I behaved after school. Before I went to the art room, I stopped at the locker I shared with Claire. She was already gone. She'd fixed a mirror to the inside of the door at the beginning of the year. I combed my hair, glossed my lips, and regretted that I hadn't worn any eye makeup that day. I didn't usually wear much makeup to school. I rarely got up early enough to take the time to put it on. Well, maybe tonight I'd set my alarm half an hour ahead.

I entered the art room with some trepidation. Mr. Wolleck was up front, working at his desk. A bunch of juniors and seniors were sitting around a table at the back. I knew many of them by sight, but they certainly didn't know me. Geoff was seated at the head of the table, trying to get them to keep quiet, when he noticed me standing in the doorway. "Hi, Dinah," he called out. "Come on, join us."

All the chairs were taken. I pulled one over from a nearby easel, placed it a little beyond the crowd, and sat down. No one else noticed me. They all seemed to be yelling at one another.

Geoff banged on the table. "Okay, okay," he said, "let's not fight the same old battles all over again. We have to make some decisions. The dance is only two weeks away."

"But I like red, white, and blue," said Claudia Santora. "What else do you use around Washington's birthday?"

Geoff's shoulders sagged. "Claudia, we vetoed red, white, and blue last time, remember? We put it to a vote. It was six to one."

"I notice no one else has come up with a decent idea," she remarked primly.

"My idea is good," said Phil Doyle. His presence on the committee surprised me even more than Geoff's had. Maybe Geoff would have seen my amazement as further evidence of my narrow-mindedness, but I think it was fair to assume that hoods were even less likely to decorate gyms than jocks. Phil had been booted off the football team the previous November for giving Coach Osinski the finger in front of a stadiumful of fans. Talk of that incident entertained the school for a week, releasing a flood of Phil Doyle stories stretching back to his kindergarten days. Phil Doyle dumping the contents of the paste pot into his third-grade teacher's pocketbook. Phil Doyle "borrowing" a video recorder from the AVA room. Phil Doyle tearing up his report card and setting fire to the scraps in the schoolyard. Phil Doyle joyriding in a Porsche lifted from Dr. MacPherson's parking lot, and then regaling the cops who picked him up with a fantastic tale about being kidnapped by creatures from another planet. I had no idea how many of the other Phil Doyle stories were true, but I'd witnessed the finger with my own eyes.

Claudia, hands on her hips, leaned her face so close to Phil's their noses almost touched. "Turn the whole gym into a Chinese opium den? For a Student Council Dance? I think that's the most awful idea I ever heard!"

Edie Hockenberry agreed. "Dr. Krinick would kill us if we did anything like that."

"We wouldn't *say* it was an opium den, stupid," Phil replied. "We'd just say it was Chinese."

"Who are you calling stupid?" Edie shot back. "You're the stupid one."

"Will you stop this?" Geoff cried. "Will you stop acting like a bunch of kindergartners?"

Chastened, Edie and Phil leaned back in their seats. All the people who'd been talking at once suddenly shut up. The unexpected silence was thick as fog.

"How about some flowers?" I suggested. I could hear my voice echoing in my own ears. "We can make those huge Mexican-style paper flowers out of colored tissue paper. They're easy to do and they're big, so we'll be able to fill up that monstrous space. We'll have a garden, a bright tropical garden. We'll make spring come a whole month early."

Every head turned. Every pair of eyes stared at me. I think it was the first moment most of them, except for Geoff, realized I was there. Struck dumb by my unexpected daring, I pressed my lips so tightly together even a breath had difficulty escaping. "Go on, Dinah," Geoff urged quietly.

"All right," I said, relaxing beneath the warmth of his gaze. "Columns around the edges of the gym—tall fluted white columns. We'll make them out of cardboard, and twine green vines around them. We'll hang huge bunches of flowers from the ceiling and we'll put great big bouquets in between the columns. A riot of color—hot colors, red, orange, yellow, and shocking pink everywhere. You know, like a boffo punch in winter's face." I had opened my sketch pad and was drawing as I spoke. "Quantity, that's what we have to go for. Architecturally, the gym is your basic Middle American Ugly. These paper flowers are a simple way of just covering all that up."

The kids sitting near me were leaning over, staring as my soft pencil flew over the page. In addition to some flowers, I sketched in a couple of leaf-entwined columns. Claudia, Phil, and Geoff came from the other end of the table and stood behind me, watching. "I thought you were no good at decorations," Geoff said softly.

"This isn't decorations. It's an idea."

"That's what we needed. An idea."

"And someone who could draw it," Phil added. "So that stupid people would understand what it's supposed to look like."

Claudia ignored his jibe. "I still like red, white, and blue," she said. "But maybe it is kind of ordinary. This is different." She tapped her finger on my sketch pad. "There's probably never been a dance at Lenape High that looked like this."

"All we need for the flowers are tissue paper and wire. They're cheap enough. The columns," I admitted, "may be more of a problem."

"I don't think it'll be so easy to shape columns six or eight feet tall out of cardboard," Steve Abruzzi said. "It's too stiff."

"Listen," Phil interjected, "I work part-time at Carpet City. The boss'll give me some of those big tubes the carpet comes rolled on. Then all we'll have to do is paint them white."

"With gray lines," I said. "To make them look fluted."

Peggy Chen picked up the sheet of paper and examined it closely. "We'll spray the tubes," she said. "You put in the fluting."

"We'll have to mount them on some kind of base," Geoff said. "So they won't fall over."

"It's a lot of work," Peggy said. "But it'll be a knockout."

Everyone else was talking, too. Only they weren't quarreling the way they had when I'd first come in. They were bubbling over with ideas. Peggy jotted down what they were saying. I guess she'd been chosen committee secretary.

"I'm pretty sure I can have the tubes here by Thursday," Phil said.

"Good," Geoff said. "We'll meet again on Thursday. Plan to stay late, because we'll start working." He put his hand on my shoulder. His gesture was so unexpected that I felt a tremor run down my arm. My hand shook, my pencil dropped from my fingers and rolled on the floor. He leaned down to pick it up. "Dinah," he asked, "can you stay a little longer?"

My tongue seemed thick as a sponge in my mouth. I replied with a nod.

"You and I can go down to the gym. We'll measure

and then you can draw a detailed plan, on graph paper. I mean, if that's all right with you."

"Yes," I murmured. "It's all right with me." I turned to Peggy. "Can I have your notes? So I can incorporate everyone's ideas into the design."

"Not everyone's," Claudia said. "No Chinese opium den."

"And no red, white, and blue," Phil shouted.

Claudia laughed. Then Phil laughed, too.

Geoff took a tape measure and several sheets of graph paper out of the closet. I grabbed my sketch book and pencil, and we headed for the gym. Something was going on in the gym all day, every day. That afternoon the girls' basketball team was practicing. But we explained our mission to Coach Arnell, and she said we could measure if we stayed away from the center of the gym floor and didn't mind risking a ball or two bouncing off our heads.

We paced the perimeter of the gym, Geoff rolling out his tape measure, I marking down the feet and inches he called out. When we were done, we stood outside in the hall to escape the noise of basketballs dribbling and Coach Arnell trumpeting out directions in the voice of a crazed elephant.

"It's a big gym," I said. "Tell Phil to get as many of those cardboard tubes as he can."

Geoff tapped the graph paper. "We really do need this plan by the next meeting on Thursday. I know that doesn't give you much time, but we don't have much time."

"I can do it." I slipped the graph paper into my sketch book. "The only thing I want to know is why you got started so late."

"Would you believe," he explained, "today was actually our third meeting? I couldn't get those guys to agree on anything. I was sure we were going to end up with nothing more than a couple of streamers and balloons. Now, all of a sudden, they love one another."

"We'll need lots of streamers," I said. "The flowers alone won't be enough to lower that ceiling. But not red,

33

white, and blue streamers. Red, orange, pink, and yellow streamers."

"The afternoon of the dance, I'll rope in a few fellows from the team," he responded. "They can hang the stuff from the ceiling. That doesn't take any talent."

"I'll get Claire and Charlie and whoever else I can think of," I said. "With enough hands we'll get it all up in a couple of hours."

He nodded. "Come on, Dinah. I'll drive you home."

In the car, just he and I in the front seat, my hands were sweating so much I had to take off my mittens. But I managed to chatter on about the decorations so coolly you'd think boys drove me home from school five afternoons a week, and picked me up five mornings, for that matter. "I didn't invent this whole idea," I said. "Like the columns—I didn't make up the columns."

"What do you mean, you didn't make them up? Of course, you didn't make them up. I think the Egyptians invented columns, about six thousand years ago."

"Egyptians, Greeks, whoever," I returned with a shrug. "I stole those columns from the ballroom at the Clover Lake Country Club. That's where we're having my brother's bar mitzvah reception."

"Tell me something, Dinah." I sensed that if he weren't driving, he would have turned to look at me. "What's so important about a bar mitzvah?"

I was surprised. There weren't huge numbers of Jews in Lenape, but there were enough to support a good-sized synagogue. Non-Jewish school friends had come to both my bat mitzvah service and my party, and Jonathan had invited several to his. "When you were in seventh grade, you didn't go to any? You didn't have any Jewish friends who invited you?"

"I went to one or two, but I didn't really understand what was going on."

"It's a ceremony that takes place on a Sabbath close to your thirteenth birthday, and it means you assume the obligations and duties of an adult Jew."

He nodded. "Like confirmation for the Catholics."

"Sort of. Only it's a bigger deal, because you do it alone." I searched for the words to convey the importance of the occasion, as I remembered my own bat mitzvah—to which Geoff Ruggles certainly had not been invited. "Each Saturday Jews read a portion of the Torah. That's our name for the first five books of the Bible. It takes a year to get through the whole thing, and then we start over again. For each portion of the Torah, there's a matching portion which also gets read, from one of the other biblical books. That's called the *haftarah*. Now the kid who's being bar mitzvahed has to read that section. In Hebrew. And he doesn't read it, actually. He chants it. If you're a real whiz, like my brother Jonathan, you end up doing a lot of psalms and prayers and stuff, too."

"In Hebrew."

"In Hebrew."

"It's tough to be Jewish."

I laughed. "You sound like my grandfather. He's always saying, '*Es ist schwer zu sein eh Yid.*' It's hard to be a Jew."

"That's Hebrew?"

"No, that's Yiddish." I sighed. "It's not only hard to be a Jew, it's complicated. Hebrew is the holy language. It's also the language they speak in Israel. But the Jews of eastern Europe didn't speak Hebrew every day. They spoke a German dialect that was written with Hebrew characters. *That's* Yiddish. My great-grandparents all came from eastern Europe. From Poland, actually."

"My grandmother was born in England," Geoff said. "She was a war bride. She has stories—you know, they're so funny and so sad at the same time. I keep telling my mom she should tape them."

I nodded. "Before it's too late. Listen, if your mom doesn't get around to it, you do it yourself. I saw a program on TV about war brides last year. I'd love to hear your grandmother's stories."

"You will," he said. "Soon."

I had made the remark casually. It was just conversa-

35

tion. But his reply seemed significant. Or was I letting that foolish elf, hope, take over again? Slowly, deliberately, I pulled on one mitten, and then the other. It was something to do.

He nosed the car into the curb in front of my house. I reached for the door handle. "Thanks for the lift, Geoff," I said. "I'll see you in art class."

He put his hand on my arm. "Dinah, wait a minute."

I shivered, the way I had earlier, at the meeting. Perhaps this time he felt my tremor. I looked into his eyes, he looked into mine, and I felt my heartbeat speed up to a million miles an hour. "Listen, Dinah," he said, "Phil and Claudia are going bowling Saturday night. You want to double?"

"Phil and Claudia? I thought they hated each other."

"They also love each other. Why do you think Phil's on a dance decorating committee? Just so he can get an extra couple of hours each week with Claudia."

"Oh." I felt pretty stupid not to have recognized that the sparks between them were a good deal more than temper.

"So do you want to come?" he repeated.

"With you?"

He regarded me quizzically. "I hope with me. You think I'm asking for someone else?"

"Thank you, Geoff," I replied firmly. "I would like to come. Very much."

"Great! We'll work out the details later."

"Good-bye, Geoff." Finally, I opened the door.

"See you tomorrow," he called. I stood on the sidewalk waving until he pulled away. And then I think I actually skipped up the path. Anyone observing me would have thought they were looking at an oversized six-year-old.

As it turned out, someone did see me, but I didn't find that out until dinnertime. By then, I'd ceased skipping. Second thoughts had settled in. Sooner or later, I'd have to tell Gram and Gramps I was going on a date with Geoff Ruggles. But I knew how they felt about Jewish kids going out with kids who weren't Jewish. In their minds, the first date was followed instantly by the Wedding March. Intermarriage, and its inevitable precursor, interdating, had been a topic of dinner conversation at our table often enough. It was only Tuesday. When I did tell them, I'd make it sound casual, like a whole bunch of us were going bowling together. Maybe that was cowardly, but the longer I postponed the announcement, the less time there'd be for lectures. I knew my grandmother. She wouldn't let even one little date get by her.

However, the matter was taken out of my hands. Mom was still in Boston, so it was just the four of us, eating in the kitchen. Casually, as he helped himself to a baked potato, Jonathan remarked, "Some guy drove you home this afternoon."

Gram and Gramps nailed me with their eyes.

"How do you know?" I asked.

"I passed you on my bike. Boy, you were so busy with him, you didn't even see me. Who was he?" Jonathan asked.

"Geoff Ruggles," I replied, as calmly as I could.

"Geoff Ruggles the quarterback?"

"The same."

"Wow!"

"All he did was drive me home, Jonathan. Don't make a federal case out of it."

"Geoff Ruggles," Gram said. "Ruggles. He's not Jewish, is he?"

She hadn't wasted any time. "No, Gram, he isn't."

"I didn't think so." She looked at Gramps and Gramps looked at her.

"You know how we feel," Gramps said. He made it sound as if Geoff belonged to another species, like maybe orangutan. "We don't think you should start something you can't finish."

"You're ridiculous!" I exclaimed. "All he did was drive me home. He didn't ask me to marry him."

"One thing leads to another," Gram said.

"Perhaps not in this case?" Gramps's heavy-lidded dark

eyes gazed at me gently. He was giving me a chance to get off the hook.

But, of course, I couldn't take it. Because one thing had already led to another. "We're going bowling Saturday night," I admitted.

"Dinah," Gram said, "the best thing will be to tell him tomorrow that you can't go. Don't make a mistake. You're not allowed to date boys who aren't Jewish."

"Not allowed?" I cried. "Not *allowed*? When was that rule invented?"

"You know our position," Gramps said. "We've spoken about our fears of intermarriage often enough."

"But Gramps, a position isn't a rule." I tried to make my voice sound reasonable. He was easier to talk to than Gram anyway. She was all emotion. At least he had the ability to think logically. "I told you. I'm not marrying him. For heaven's sake, I'm not even sixteen years old."

"I met your grandfather when I was sixteen," Gram reminded me. "I didn't marry him until I was twenty, but I never went with anyone else."

"Gram, I'm not you."

"Of course you're not, but that's not the point," Gramps said. "I know you'll probably go out with dozens of boys before you pick the one you want to marry. But if you get in the habit of going with gentiles, you could end up marrying a gentile. Like I said, it's just best not to start something you can't finish."

"Because if every Jew marries a gentile, pretty soon there won't be any Jews left," Gram said. "There aren't a whole lot of us as it is."

"Just because I want to go bowling with Geoff Ruggles, suddenly I personally am responsible for the potential demise of the entire Jewish people?" The thought was almost funny. "I mean, that's nonsense, Gram, and you know it."

"The Jewish people is made up of individual Jews," Gramps said quietly. "The actions of each one affect all. Just because we feel comfortable and secure in this country doesn't mean we can ever forget what happened in Nazi

Germany, or what's happening now in Russia and other parts of the world."

I felt as if the conversation had gotten way out of hand. "Look," I said, "Geoff is the first guy who's ever asked me out. Do you realize that? The very first guy. And it's not as if he's some nerd. My very first real date is going to be with this absolutely terrific person. And you want me to turn him down. You're crazy. I won't do it. I mean, to keep me home Saturday night, you'd have to lock me in my room." They'd never do that. It wasn't their style. "And then," I added, just to make sure, "I'd climb out the window."

"Ridiculous!" Gram spit the word out of her mouth. "No one's chaining you to your bed. We're just asking you to be sensible."

"The sensible thing to do is go out with him," I assured her. "I mean, you'd have to be utterly insensible not to go out with Geoff Ruggles if he asked you."

Gramps sighed. "Dinah, I thought you cared about being Jewish. I really did. You took your bat mitzvah so seriously, and you continued with Hebrew high school afterward, and you go to temple youth group meetings—"

"One of those boys," Gram interrupted. "Why don't you go bowling Saturday night with one of those boys?" From her tone, you'd think she'd just stumbled on a notion worthy of the Nobel prize.

"Gram," I said, "*those* boys don't ask me."

That shut her up. Maybe I'd told her about the Paul Levy incident. She knew no Jewish boy had ever asked me.

It didn't look as if anyone was going to eat anything else. I stood up and began clearing the table. "Your mother will hear about this," Gram said.

"Of course my mother will hear about this." She called most nights when she was away, but she might not tonight because she was coming home the next day. "You don't have to tell her. I'll tell her myself." I thought my mother might possibly be pleased. I'd finally achieved what she'd wanted for me ever since I'd gotten into high school—a date.

39

She arrived late the next afternoon. Gram was at the JINS shelter, Gramps was taking his daily five-mile constitutional, and Jonathan was at Hebrew school. I was glad I was home alone. I wanted to get to her before Gram did.

After we'd hugged and kissed and she'd told me that things had gone well in Boston, I put the kettle on for tea. "Let's sit for a few minutes, Mom," I said. "I want to talk to you."

"Good. I want to talk to you, too."

I took a seat facing her. "I mean I have something specific to tell you."

"Oh? Go ahead. I'm all ears."

I got right to the point. "I have a date Saturday night."

"Hey, that's super!"

I'd known she'd say that. "Gramps isn't very happy about it."

"Really, in effect Gramps has been your father, and you know fathers. You should have seen what he put poor Allie Moscowitz through." I'd heard the story of Allie Moscowitz, my mother's first boyfriend, before. "Gramps gave him a driving test before he'd let me get in Allie's car."

"It wasn't just Gramps. Gram hit the ceiling, too, even worse," I explained. "It's not Geoff's car or his driving. It has nothing to do with him personally. They don't even know him. It's because he isn't Jewish."

"Oh." The amused expression disappeared from my mother's face. "What did Gram say? That she'd mourn you as if you were dead if you married a man who wasn't Jewish?"

"Well, not quite, but almost. Mom, I'm not going to marry Geoff. We're just going bowling."

"You have to understand how they feel. They think it's best not to start . . ."

"What you can't finish," I chanted, in unison with her.

"I feel that way, too," Mom said.

I'd hoped for a different reaction. "I didn't really expect that from you. From Gramps, from Gram, maybe. But from you?"

"I'm as interested as they are in having a Jewish home, in raising Jewish children."

"Well, you do have a Jewish home, and you do have Jewish children. I can't see what that has to do with my going bowling with Geoff Ruggles." I leaned forward, as if somehow, by getting close to her, I could make her understand. "Oh, Mom, he's wonderful. Not only handsome and popular and a good athlete and all that stuff, but just so nice. I still can't believe he's interested in me. It's like a miracle."

Slowly, she shook her head. "Darling, I can't stick you in your playpen to keep you out of trouble, the way I could when you were two. But I think it's important for you to know how I feel. I would rather you dated Jewish boys."

"All right, Mom," I returned sharply. "You expressed your opinion. Now I'm going to express mine. I'm surprised at what you're saying. I always thought you'd be pleased if I started going out."

Her hands folded under her chin, she gazed at me with worried eyes. "It's you I'm concerned about. When you get involved with boys from backgrounds different than yours, it just creates extra problems, problems you don't need." She smiled a little. "It's tough enough for a man and a woman to connect across the barrier of sex without throwing in other complications."

I pulled out the argument I'd used the night before. "Geoff asked me. What Jewish boy has ever asked me?"

Mom sighed. "Look, Dinah, I told you. I can't lock you in a cage. I just want you to know how I feel."

"You'll meet him Saturday night," I said. "You'll see how wonderful he is. Then maybe you'll feel different. I'm sure you will."

I didn't know about Gram. Maybe she'd never feel different. But she wasn't my parent. Mom was. What she thought mattered most. Or at least that was what I was telling myself.

FOUR

The doorbell rang exactly at seven-thirty Saturday night. I was ready. I'd been getting ready since five. Claire had come over carrying half her wardrobe and a box of makeup in case I wanted to borrow something from her. In the end, I took a pair of bright pink earrings, because they exactly matched the bulky cotton knit sweater I was wearing, and some pink lipstick that matched, too. I thought I looked pretty good. It's amazing what someone else's interest can do for your attitude toward yourself. A week ago I'd been convinced I was about as attractive as a giraffe. Now it seemed to me that the eye for color and style I'd always possessed had produced a girl who was, if not exactly beautiful, certainly well enough put together.

I rushed for the door. I didn't want anyone opening it but me. For February, the night was very warm, maybe fifty degrees, and the air smelled damp and sweet, like spring. When I saw him standing there in front of me, his broad shoulders threatening to rip through his denim jacket, I felt a sudden surge of joy. This wasn't the art room, this wasn't the gym, this wasn't the library. This was my first real date, and it was with a guy I was crazy about. I was undeservedly, insanely lucky. If I'd known what was waiting for me at the end of all those years of hanging around, I'd have been more patient. "Hi, Geoff," I said.

"Hi, Dinah." He smiled, as if he was as pleased to see me as I was to see him.

"The clan has gathered," I said. "They want to meet you."

"That sounds a little scary." He grabbed my hand. "But if you hold on to me, it'll give me courage." His fingers squeezing mine gave me courage, too.

I led him into the family room. They were all there, settling in to eat popcorn and watch the two videos Gramps had brought home. Gram sat in her Eames Chair with her tablecloth spread out on her lap and a box of brightly colored embroidery silks on the table next to her. Now she was working on a sprig of purple lilac, symbolizing first love, according to her flower dictionary.

My mother was sitting there, too, preparing to spend a Saturday night at home. She'd broken up with Sam Midman, her most recent boyfriend, and no one had yet appeared to replace him. But someone would, soon enough. They always did.

"Folks," I said, "I'd like you to meet my friend, Geoff Ruggles. Geoff, these are my grandparents, Mr. and Mrs. Horowitz, and my mother, Mrs. Adler. And this character over here is my brother, Jonathan."

Geoff extended his hand. "Hi, Mr. Horowitz." Gramps shook it briefly. "Hi, Mrs. Horowitz." Gram barely nodded.

Mom stood up. "It's very nice to meet you, Geoff," she said, extending her own hand. One star for Mom. She may not have been enthusiastic about my going out with Geoff, but at least she wasn't going to embarrass me in front of him.

"I saw the Thanksgiving game," Jonathan said. "I saw your fifty-five-yard run. That was something."

"Yeah, well, thanks," Geoff said. "It would have been more something if we'd won."

"It wasn't your fault," Jonathan said.

"It's always the quarterback's fault."

43

"Well, next year," Jonathan suggested.

Geoff laughed. "Certainly next year. Do you play football?"

"He does not," Gram said thinly. "We'd never permit it."

"I don't have the build," Jonathan explained. "And I don't think I ever will. I think you can tell by the time you're thirteen."

"Well, maybe," Geoff said. He eyed Jonathan critically. "But you don't know yet how tall you're going to be. So maybe basketball. Or baseball."

"He plays tennis," Gram said.

"Tennis is a good game," Geoff said. "I like it a lot. Maybe we can hit a few balls sometime."

Jonathan glanced at Gram. "I don't play tennis *well*," he said.

Geoff grinned. "Neither do I. One day when the weather gets nice, I'll take you on in the park."

Jonathan grinned, too, and nodded.

"Jonathan is very busy," Gram said.

"Not too busy to play tennis," Mom interjected. "Tennis is good for Jonathan."

The family room seemed to have turned into a shrinking box, with walls pressing in on me. I glanced at my watch. "Well," I announced, "we have to go. Some friends are waiting for us." I made it sound as if they were out in the car, though I knew they weren't. We were to pick them up on our way to the bowling alley.

"Good-bye," Geoff said. "It was nice to meet all of you."

Gram said nothing. Gramps nodded. Mom smiled.

"It sure was nice to meet *you*," Jonathan said. He and Geoff shook hands.

We hurried out of the house and into the car. Geoff concentrated on starting the engine and pulling out of the driveway, while I concentrated on keeping my mouth shut. It was not until we were out on the road that he spoke. "Anyway," he said, "your brother liked me."

44

So he'd noticed. Well, only a creature with all the sensitivity of an oyster could have missed Gram's coldness. And as I'd learned, Geoff's feelings were as easily hurt as anyone's—as easily as mine, for example. "Mom liked you. And Gramps didn't *not* like you," I said.

"But your grandmother hated me. Why?" He sounded surprised. If Geoff ran for president of Lenape High, maybe three people would have voted against him. He wasn't accustomed to hostile encounters.

I told him the truth. "It's because you're not Jewish."

"Because I'm not Jewish!" he repeated in a tone of absolute astonishment. "You mean your grandmother won't let you have friends who aren't Jewish? What's the matter with her? She doesn't *look* old-fashioned."

"My grandmother's very modern," I retorted defensively. "Claire isn't Jewish. She's my friend, and Gram loves her."

"So what's wrong with me?"

"You're a boy."

"No kidding."

"She doesn't like my dating a non-Jewish boy." I didn't tell him Mom wasn't crazy about it, either, only more polite. "She thinks interdating leads to intermarriage which leads to the demise of the Jewish people."

"Pretty heavy."

I nodded.

"I didn't ask you to marry me. I only asked you to go bowling."

"Yes, that's what I told her. It didn't make any difference." I put my hand on his sleeve. "Listen, Geoff, that's my grandmother. That's not me. Let's forget about her."

"You don't feel the way she does?"

"If I did, would I be here?"

"Okay," he agreed. "Then we'll forget about it."

We pulled up in front of Claudia's house. "I'll go and get her," Geoff said. "You can wait here."

"I don't mind going in," I offered. "You can stay be-

45

hind the wheel." Geoff was really polite. Claudia wasn't his date. Another boy would have just blown the horn.

"No, no," he insisted. "I'll go. I have to." Before I could say another word, he popped out of the car and hurried up the path. Claudia must have been watching for him, because no more than ninety seconds later they walked out of the house together.

They climbed into the car. "We'll pick up Phil now," Geoff said.

"Where's his house?" I asked.

"Bartine Street."

"Bartine Street?" I'd lived in Lenape all my life, but I didn't know Bartine Street.

"It's on the east side," Claudia explained.

We drove past the abandoned textile mills, rows of narrow houses with dirty white front steps, and rundown four-story brick tenements. Phil lived in a tract of small ranch houses that had been built just after World War II. In sharp contrast to the streets through which we had just passed, most of the homes proclaimed the attentiveness of their owners. Phil's was no different. It appeared to have been refaced recently with siding of imitation gray brick. A neat white fence surrounded the tiny lot. Bushes were thick around the foundation and vines climbed the fence. It was winter and most plants were leafless, but even so I could tell that Phil's front yard was someone's cherished garden.

This time Geoff blew the horn. Phil seemed to leap out of the front door and into the car, throwing his arm around Claudia and planting a large, loud kiss on her cheek. "Hello, sweetheart," he said.

"Careful, Phil, you'll mess my hair," she protested. But she was laughing at the same time.

"You're irresistible, didn't you know that? Let your hair take care of itself." This time he gave her a real kiss, a long, lingering one on the lips. Looking at them, I felt like a Peeping Tom. Quickly, I turned away and stared out of the windshield in front of me.

Geoff covered the moment with chatter. "Which bowling alley do you like better, Strike and Spare or Bowlerama? Strike and Spare is bigger and newer, but Bowlerama is probably less crowded."

"I'm not much of a bowler, Geoff." Bowling and roller-skating were things we'd done in crowds on Saturdays or school holidays when we were in junior high. I hadn't gone near an alley or a rink since I'd left eighth grade. "I mean, I enjoy it, but I'm not very good at it. It certainly doesn't make any difference to me where we go. You pick."

"No point in asking them," he said lightly, with a movement of his head toward the backseat.

"I hear every word you're saying," Phil announced. He and Claudia must have decided to come up for air. "I vote for Bowlerama."

"I vote for Strike and Spare," said Claudia. "The food at Bowlerama is inedible. They never change the grease in their fry machine."

"Bowlerama," Phil insisted. "We're not going there to eat. We're going there to bowl."

"I'm driving," Geoff said. "I'll make the decision." Apparently, he was used to them. He didn't take their quarrels seriously.

We went to Bowlerama. I was an even worse bowler than I'd remembered. But Geoff didn't seem to mind. He kept giving me pointers. He was a good teacher. He made it clear we were there to have fun, not win games, and slowly I found myself relaxing. By the end of the evening, I was knocking down a few pins with each roll. Every time that happened, Geoff praised me so extravagantly you'd think I'd just won the decathlon at the Olympics. He made me laugh.

As a bowler, Geoff, though unpracticed, was all right, because he was an athlete. Phil was better, and Claudia was by far the best of the four of us. She really knew the game. She told me her father had once come in third in the New Jersey State bowling championships, and had given her a little ball and her first lessons when she was six. Of course, she and Phil beat me and Geoff every game, even though they seemed to expend most of their energy reaming each other out for what each claimed was the other's incredibly stupid mistakes.

We didn't eat at the bowling alley. Claudia absolutely refused, and for once Phil didn't argue with her. He and Geoff seemed no more anxious to nibble potatoes fried in rancid oil than she did. We drove to Alphonso's for pizza.

We ran into some juniors and seniors, and sat with them—eight of us squeezed into a booth. I didn't have much to say, but I wasn't actually uncomfortable. Geoff sat next to me, his arm draped around the back of the booth behind me. Everyone was friendly. I was with Geoff; I belonged.

Peggy Chen seemed to be Claudia's particular friend. "Any trouble tonight when Phil picked you up?" she asked.

Claudia shook her head. "He didn't pick me up. Geoff did. Geoff came in the house. They thought he was my date."

"What are you going to do the night of the dance?" Peggy wanted to know.

"The same thing, I guess." She touched Geoff's shoulder. "Is that okay with you?"

Geoff shifted himself closer to me, frowning a little.

"I really appreciate it," Claudia said so softly I had to lean forward to catch her words. "It saves me so much hassle. I'll pay you back one day, Geoff, really I will."

"You don't need to pay me back," Geoff said. "That's not the point."

She sighed. "I know." Suddenly her brows lifted on a question. "Oh, my gosh. You *are* going to the dance, aren't you? After all the work you've done, you are going."

He turned to me and looked into my eyes. "Am I?" he asked.

My heart did a triple somersault. "What do you mean?" I replied in a low voice, so only he could hear. Though I knew my question probably sounded pretty stupid, I wasn't going to risk any misunderstandings.

He smiled. "Am I going with you?"

"Yes. If you want to."

"That's why I asked. Because I want to."

I smiled, too. I couldn't look at him any longer. His eyes were too dazzling. I turned away and lifted a piece of pizza from the platter in the middle of the table. But I didn't actually eat. I couldn't do that, either.

We dropped Phil at his house first. Claudia walked him in, and it was a while before she came back. Geoff and I waited in the car. "Usually," I said, "the guy walks the girl home. What's going on around here?"

"Claudia's folks don't like Phil," Geoff said. "They forbid Claudia to go out with him. That's why I pick her up. They think she's dating me now. It's a mess, and I hate being in the middle of it."

"Boy, so would I."

"But what can I do?" Geoff glanced out the window at Phil's house and then turned back to me. "I live three doors down from Claudia; she's been my friend since we were in diapers. And Phil's a pal, too."

"You're not much alike." I kept my tone neutral.

"Phil and I got to be friends on the football team. Coach Osinski really gives it to the freshman guys. He thinks he's a drill sergeant, but he just couldn't get to Phil. Phil taught me how to take it. I'd have never made it on the team without him."

"But Phil didn't make it," I pointed out.

"I guess one of the things I learned from Phil was never to go as far as he does." He paused for a moment, frowning. "With Phil, what starts out as fooling around ends up as a major confrontation. He can't stand adults telling him what to do. And yet, a guy his own age couldn't ask for a better friend."

"So that's why Claudia's family hates him so much," I commented. "Because he's a wise guy."

"He's so crazy about Claudia, I'm sure he never mouthed off to them. He's hardly mouthed off to anyone, really, since he started going with her." The streetlamp lit the

49

interior of the car, and I could see his eyes, serious and thoughtful. "I think Phil is really an okay guy. He hasn't had it easy. He never mentions his father. He lives with his mom and his grandmother. His grandmother works on an assembly line, and his mother is a waitress at the Sunset Diner."

I didn't have a father. I lived with my mother and my grandmother. But I did have a grandfather, and my mother wasn't a waitress in a diner, and like Geoff and Claudia, we lived in the best neighborhood in town. "None of that stuff has anything to do with Phil," I protested.

"You don't have to persuade *me*," Geoff said. "It's the Santoras who have to be persuaded. They know Phil's reputation. He's on probation because of that business with Dr. MacPherson's Porsche. It was the talk of St. Mary's."

"If they all go to church . . ." I began.

"Phil's grandmother's a big churchgoer, and so are the Santoras. Mr. Santora is a deacon."

At least Phil and Claudia were both Catholic. His religion was one thing the Santoras couldn't hold against him. "What's a deacon?" I wondered.

"That's as high as a layperson can go in the Catholic church. But Phil and his mom just go Christmas and Easter, I guess. Like me."

"Are your folks Catholic?" I asked.

"We go to Archangel Lutheran when we go," Geoff said. "Each one of my grandparents grew up a different kind of Protestant."

I felt relieved. I suspected it might be easier to sell my family on a Protestant than a Catholic. But then I was annoyed with myself for my relief, because it had come for all the wrong reasons. "Phil isn't into anything now, is he?" I asked. "I mean anything really rough."

"I don't think so," Geoff returned slowly. "But I don't know everything that goes on with Phil. He's got some friends from his neighborhood. They're older. I just don't know."

"The Santoras don't know, either," I said. "They're judging him without knowing."

"Well, maybe they could be perfectly tolerant of Phil if he were just some kid they knew. But he wants to be their daughter's boyfriend. Actually, he *is* her boyfriend, though they don't know it." I admired Geoff's ability to see both Phil's and the Santoras' points of view. "Claudia's their darling," he continued. "They've always treated her as if she were made out of glass."

"Claudia?"

He laughed. "It's funny, all right. Because what she's really made out of is carbon steel. But they don't realize that, either. Fathers can be sort of nervous about daughters. I have a sister. I know."

"I don't know," I said. "My dad died when I was three."

"That's tough."

I shrugged. "Mom's done okay by us. And we have Gram and Gramps. I didn't even know him, so how can I miss him?" But then I added truthfully, "I guess I do, though. Not him in particular. Just the idea of a father. Jonathan does, too."

"I understand," he said quietly. And I believed that he did.

Claudia had escorted Phil into the house. Phil returned the favor and escorted her back to the car. She didn't seem to care any longer that the hairdo she'd earlier protected so assiduously was now a mess. Clinging to Phil as they stood on the curb, she kissed him again.

Geoff rolled down the window. "You can go back in by yourself, Phil," he said. "Otherwise we'll be here all night with the two of you marching up and down."

Phil opened the rear door. Claudia climbed in, and then he shut it. He waved, she blew a kiss, and Geoff pulled away. I turned my head and glanced at her in the backseat. Laughing, teasing, quarrelsome Claudia was still and sober as a tombstone angel.

Geoff walked her to her door. I watched him give her cheek a friendly peck, and then return to the car. "Except that I'm not Catholic, Claudia's parents think I'm the most wonderful boyfriend a daughter of theirs could have," he commented dryly as he started the car up again. "So polite, so respectful. No making out in the front parlor. Scarcely even a good-night kiss on the porch."

"Do you think they're watching?" I asked.

"I wouldn't put it past them."

"How do they know you don't do your making out in the car?"

His head turned toward me for a split second. Then his eyes were back on the road. "Well, Dinah," he said softly, "they don't know, do they?"

My mouth was suddenly dry, my hands damp and clammy. I hadn't felt nervous since I'd rolled my first bowling ball down the alley three hours before. But now again there was a hollowness in the pit of my stomach. He was probably going to kiss me. I could figure out that much. But then what would I do? I'd read a lot of books, but my knowledge was almost entirely academic. We'd played kissing games at parties when I was in sixth grade. That was the extent of my actual experience. Suppose he kissed me and then was sorry that he'd ever asked me to the Student Council Dance. I'd wish I was right back where I had been a week ago, Dinah Adler, the girl who'd never gone out with a guy.

But it was okay. It was more than okay. It was lovely. He parked the car in front of my house and turned to me. "Dinah, let's say good night here. All right?" I didn't say anything. I was sure if I did my voice would tremble. I just nodded.

He put his arm around me and pulled me to him. His face moved closer and closer, filling my vision, and then I shut my eyes. His lips touched mine, gently, tentatively. I shivered. He felt it, and held me tighter. I put my arms around his neck and kissed him back. I did know what to do, after all.

He walked me to the door. "I'll call you tomorrow," he said.

"You don't have to. We'll see each other Monday."

His eyes narrowed. "I want to."

"Okay."

He kissed me again, this time on the cheek, and said good night. I unlocked the door, floated inside, and wafted up the stairs. In my room I took off my clothes, slowly, dreamily, dropping each garment on the chair and then proceeding to the next one as languorously as if I were in a slow-motion movie. I wasn't thinking. I was reliving those moments in the car when we'd had our arms around each other, and feeling the sensations I'd felt then all over again.

I put on one of the long T-shirts I slept in and stepped out into the hall. Kiss or no kiss, I had to brush my teeth. Gram came out of her room. She was wearing a nightgown and bathrobe, but her sharp brown eyes were wide open. I knew she wasn't going to the bathroom, because she and Gramps had a bathroom attached to their bedroom. "I thought I heard you come in," she said.

"Yes," I replied briefly.

"You're not going out with him again, are you?"

"Oh, Gram," I said, "don't start in on me at midnight, please."

"You're not going out with him again." This time it was a statement.

"Yes, I am," I said. "I'm going with him to the Student Council Dance."

"He's just a football player," she snapped. "I don't know what you see in him."

Just a football player. I remembered my own surprise when I'd found out he cared about painting and drawing, when I'd discovered that his feelings were as easily hurt as anyone else's. "You don't know anything about him," I retorted.

"I know he isn't Jewish."

"Neither is Claire. Neither is Erna. Neither is Howard." Howard was Jonathan's best friend. "Neither is Mrs. Trimbach." Gram loved Phyllis Trimbach, who was one of the professional social workers at the JINS shelter. And Mrs. Trimbach was far from Gram's only non-Jewish friend.

53

"This is different," Gram insisted.

The door to Mom's bedroom opened, and she stepped out in the hall, her eyes puffy with sleep. "What's going on here?" she complained. "Is this the time or the place for a party?"

"It's no party," I replied grimly.

"I want Dinah to promise not to go out with that boy again," Gram said. At least she lowered her voice.

"Mother, I think that's my business," Mom said. "I'll take care of it. In the morning. You go to bed. Both of you."

"I'm going to the Student Council Dance with him," I repeated. "I am, I am."

"We'll talk about it in the morning."

"You can't make me not go with him."

She shot me a glance. Finally, I understood. She wasn't going to tell me it was all right to go with him in front of Gram. Maybe she wasn't going to tell me it was all right to go with him at all. But whatever her position, there was at least a chance it wasn't going to be set in concrete, like Gram's. "Go to bed, Dinah," she said.

"Okay." I marched off to the bathroom and didn't say good night to either of them. In sixteen years, I'd never been as furious with them as I was at that moment. They had cheated me. They had ruined my golden evening.

But later, in bed, I thought, "What was, was. They can't take it away from me, and I won't let them spoil the memory." I fell asleep dreaming again of Geoff's kiss.

FIVE

I slept late the next morning. Can you sleep late on purpose? Maybe I did, because by the time I got downstairs, Gram and Gramps had already left for the city where they were meeting friends for brunch and a matinee.

Mom had disappeared, too. In the kitchen, I poured myself a glass of orange juice and carried it into the family room. Jonathan, his elbows on the floor and his head resting on his hands, was stretched out on his belly reading the comics. He looked up as I entered and grinned. "I bet you had fun last night," he said.

At least there was one person in this house besides me who totally approved of Geoff. "Yes," I said. "I had fun. I had lots of fun."

Jonathan sat up. "Listen, Dinah, I want to ask you something."

"Shoot."

He hesitated a moment, his eyes fixed on the floor. Then, suddenly, he blurted out his question. "Did he kiss you?"

He was so serious, I didn't dare smile. "I think that's private information," I replied.

"I'm not asking because I'm nosy," he said. "I'm asking for a reason."

I sat cross-legged on the floor next to him. "What's the reason?"

"I want to know how to do it."

"Do what?"

"Kiss, stupid. Isn't that what we're talking about?"

"You've seen movies. Just do it that way."

"You mean with your mouth open? Isn't it kind of wet?"

"You don't have to do it with your mouth open. Not to start with." I couldn't help a small giggle. Suddenly I, Dinah Adler, was the authority on kissing. A regular teen-age Dr. Ruth. "Who're you planning to kiss, Jonathan?" I asked. I didn't believe his question had been abstract.

The corners of his mouth lifted a little. "I think that's private information."

"Well," I returned, "if I *did* do any kissing last night, you're certainly aware of whom I was doing it with."

"Maybe I just want to know in case it comes up," he returned airily. "I *am* going to be thirteen, you know. In your bar mitzvah year, you go to all these parties. . . ."

"Does your crowd ever play kissing games? I mean, they're sort of practice." I'd hated them, though. When the bottle pointed to me, the boy who'd spun it always made a face.

Apparently Jonathan didn't like them much, either. "Howard and I used to lock ourselves in the john when they played kissing games. We thought they were the dumbest things. They don't play them anymore. There's the bar mitzvah reception, and that's grown-ups' dancing. . . ."

"And boys' throwing mashed potatoes and festooning toilet paper all over the bathroom." I remembered.

"Yeah. And then there's the kids' party, and that's roller-skating or swimming or bowling."

"Then what do you need to know how to kiss for? Just stick to dancing, for the time being. Listen, I promise you, when the right moment comes, you'll figure out what to do."

He glanced at me from the corner of his eyes. "So he did kiss you."

I raised my eyebrows, bit my lower lip, and said nothing.

"Don't worry," he said. "I won't tell Mom."

Mom had probably figured it out for herself. But I didn't say that, either.

"Something funny happened last night," he continued. "I mean to Mom."

"What's that?"

"We were watching a movie when the doorbell rang. You know who it was?"

"Of course I don't."

"Guess."

"Oh, come on, Jonathan, I'm not in the mood for games."

"Guess!" He was milking this for all it was worth.

"E.T.," I said. "Lee Iacocca. The Prince of Wales. How do I know?"

"Chicken Little," he exclaimed.

"Oh, boy," I said. "What did he want her to do? Fly to Timbuktu this afternoon?"

"He just stopped by to say hello. That's what he said. He stayed for the whole rest of the movie." Jonathan sat up with his legs crossed, his elbows resting on his knees, and his face in his hands. "Chicken Little and Mom and Gram talked through most of it. Not Gramps, though; he watched with me. It started out, this dentist was murdered—"

"Forget the movie," I interrupted. "I want to hear about Chicken Little."

"He stayed for coffee. I went up to bed, and they were still sitting down here, the four of them, talking and eating."

"Well," I said, "he's known Mom so long, he really is her friend, I guess. We might not like him so much, but maybe she does."

"That's not all." His voice had dropped to a whisper, even though there wasn't another soul in the house. "I was in the bathroom, and the porch light was on. I could see him leaving. He stood by the front door down there, and he kissed her. I saw it. He kissed her." He sounded as shocked as if he'd witnessed a murder.

"That's nothing," I assured him. "Grown-ups are always kissing each other when they say hello and good-bye."

"This was a real kiss."

"I thought you didn't know anything about kissing."

"I know that much," he replied darkly.

Since he'd already evidenced considerable interest, I figured maybe this was a good time to introduce him to some of the facts of life. "Mom has had a lot of boyfriends," I said. "I'm sure she's kissed them. You have to expect that." It was only recently that I'd admitted to myself what some part of me had actually known all along—that my mother had a sex life. But feeling the way I did this morning, I was willing to grant romance to the whole world. Even to Jonathan, if that's what he wanted.

But his state of mind wasn't so generous. "I don't like it. Not with Chicken Little."

"Do you think you'd have liked it any better if you'd seen her kissing Sam Midman? I bet not."

We heard the back door slam. "Speak of the devil," Jonathan murmured.

"Hey, guys," Mom called, "help me with the groceries."

"So that's where you were," I said, as I entered the kitchen.

"Yeah, at the supermarket. I don't do enough around here. Gram isn't getting any younger, you know."

Jonathan and I helped her carry in the bundles and put the groceries away. We chattered about nothing in particular. Geoff wasn't mentioned. Neither was Mr. Chickering.

But after we were done, Mom said she wanted to talk to me.

"Go ahead, talk to her," Jonathan said.

"Alone, smart aleck," Mom said.

Jonathan struck his chest with his fist. "You have wounded me to the quick."

"This is girl talk, Jonathan," Mom said. "You'd be bored."

"I bet I wouldn't." But he left anyway.

Mom sat down at the kitchen table with a cup of coffee.

She offered me a cup, too, which was something she'd never done before. But I didn't take it. I didn't like coffee. "We have a lot to discuss," Mom said. "Gram's so worried."

I dug my heels into the rung of my chair. "I'm going to the dance with Geoff. I don't care what she thinks," I said, looking her directly in the eye. "Besides, she's not my mother. You are."

"And I'd never forbid you. That's never been the style of our relationship." Absently, she stirred her coffee with a spoon, even though she drank it black. "I don't have that power anyway. Not unless I'm willing to threaten to throw you out and cut you off without a penny, which would be an utterly ridiculous threat, because you know I'd never actually do it. But I feel much the same way Gram does. I really do. It would be better if you never got started with Geoff."

"Mom, it's already started."

"Oh, baby, you've had one date with him. You can still end it."

"I don't want to end it. Geoff is the most wonderful thing that's ever happened to me."

She let out her breath in a long sigh.

I leaned forward. "We get along, Mom," I said. "Not like some mothers and daughters. I respect you, you respect me. I don't think I've done anything to change that. Have I?"

She leaned back in her chair. "No," she replied slowly. "You haven't."

The phone rang. I leaped to my feet as if I'd been stuck with a pin. Mom sighed again.

It was Geoff, just as I'd hoped. "I didn't wake you, did I?" he asked.

"Oh, no. I've already had two long talks this morning, one with Jonathan, and one with my mother. They were both about you."

"Good things, I hope."

"Naturally," I lied.

"I had fun last night," he said softly.

"Me, too." The best time ever, I might have added.

"I could pick you up tomorrow, drive you to school."

"No, that's all right." The part of me that wanted to say yes was defeated by the part of me that didn't want to hassle my grandmother's reaction. "If Gramps is meeting his cronies at the West End Deli for breakfast, he drops me. Otherwise, I take the bus. It's nothing."

"You're sure?"

"I'm sure."

He hesitated for a moment. "Okay, then. See you tomorrow."

"Yes. Bye."

"Bye."

We hung up. My heart was singing again. It definitely looked like I had myself a boyfriend. Even I, who examined every good thing that happened like a jeweler inspecting a diamond for flaws, could recognize that. But, of course, there *was* a flaw. I wanted to drive to school with him. I wanted everyone to see me getting out of his car. For me, that would be like pulling up to the Academy Awards in a limousine. But I wasn't going to aggravate my family any more than necessary. To spare them and me some misery, I'd play it as coolly as I could. Being picked up in the morning by your boyfriend is a nice thing, but a person can live without it.

The phone rang again. Again, it was for me—this time Claire. She wanted a detailed rerun of the previous evening, which I didn't mind giving her, because there was nothing I liked better than reliving it.

"We could double," she exclaimed when she heard he was taking me to the dance. "Wouldn't that be neat?"

"We'll probably have to go with Phil and Claudia," I replied.

"Well, maybe we could triple."

"Sure, maybe we could. I'll ask."

"Oh, Dinah," she sighed, "it's so wonderful. It's just so wonderful. I'm so happy for you."

"There is a fly in the ointment," I admitted. "A small fly."

"He has bad breath. Buy him a bottle of mouthwash for his birthday."

"No, Claire, this is serious. My folks don't like him."

"Don't like Geoff! That's impossible."

"It's not that they don't like him," I amended. "I mean if they met him on the street they'd like him well enough, I guess. What they don't like is my going out with him. Because he's not Jewish."

"Oh." She sounded stunned. "You said something about that before. I didn't believe it."

"You can believe it."

"Your folks are so . . . so understanding, so up-to-date."

"In their minds, interdating leads to intermarriage, and intermarriage threatens Jewish survival."

"Oh, how ridiculous."

"No," I replied quietly, "I think I understand why it's not ridiculous. Intermarriage *is* a big problem. Even if the Jewish partner remains Jewish, the children usually aren't."

"Well, what do your folks want? To live in a ghetto?"

"No. They don't want that, either."

It was a dilemma. Talking to Claire, I suddenly understood that there were certain issues it was impossible to really share with her, even if she was my best friend. Would it bother me if Peggy Chen and every other American of Chinese extraction married a Caucasian so that a hundred years from now there were no longer any ethnic Chinese in this country? Of course not. The only people who were going to care about that were Mr. and Mrs. Chen—maybe.

After Claire and I hung up, I asked myself the real question. Did it matter to me? Yes, it mattered. Did it matter to me more than going out with Geoff did? Well, I wasn't going to stop. No abstraction could possibly matter as much as dating Geoff.

Mom took Jonathan and me out for supper. Gram and Gramps were back by the time we got home. Gram reported on her day in vivid detail, but she did not address one remark directly to me. She was mad and she was letting me know it.

Before I went upstairs, I kissed Mom good night. Then I kissed Gramps, who put his arms around me and gave me a hug. "Good night, honey," he said.

I moved over to Gram, bent down, and touched her cheek with my lips. She glanced at me, and then her eyes fell. She didn't speak. I was fifty years younger than she, but she was the one acting like a baby.

In school the next day, I was almost able to forget about them. Not that I saw so much of Geoff. I was a sophomore; he was a junior. Our paths didn't often cross. But though we spent little time together during the school day, everyone seemed to know about us. Claire and I scrutinized the details of Saturday night once more. Phil and Claudia caught up with me in the hall between math and gym and walked with me. Claudia invited me to eat lunch at her table, but I explained that I ate with Claire and a bunch of other sophomore girls. She understood. Juniors and seniors nodded and said hello to me. I knew it was only because of Geoff, but I enjoyed it anyway. I figured if fame comes your way, you should savor it while it lasts.

Erna cornered me in the library. "Can I come over tonight?" she asked. "I want to hear all about it."

I pretended not to know what she was talking about. "Hear all about what?"

"You know. You and Geoff."

"There's nothing to tell, Erna. We went bowling, that's all."

She was not so easily deflected. "But he's taking you to the Student Council Dance."

"How do you know?"

"Claire told me. It's true, isn't it?"

"Yes, it's true."

"So I want to hear. It's a romance, like in a book. It's the closest I'll ever get to a love story," she added wistfully.

"You don't know that, Erna," I said. "A year ago—a month ago—a week ago—I felt the same. You're only a freshman. You've got plenty of time." Even to my own ears I sounded like somebody's mother.

"Can I come over tonight?" she repeated. That was the trouble with Erna. Give her an inch and she grabbed the whole ruler.

"Yeah, sure," I said. But she'd get no play-by-play from me. Let Gram entertain her, Gram who was so kindhearted and understanding toward everyone except her own granddaughter.

After school, the decoration committee met. Phil had brought the cardboard tubes from the carpet store and we spent the afternoon painting them. Claudia and I were working together. "We'll double for this dance, okay?" she said.

"Can Claire and Charlie come too?" I asked.

"Sure," she said. "Why not?" She dipped her brush in the paint pot and began slapping vigorously at the column. "I appreciate it, you know."

I knew what she was talking about. My head bobbed in a small nod, but I said nothing.

"I'm sure you don't like it much," she went on. "I know Geoff hates it. But what can I do? My parents are so against Phil, and I love him so much. I guess I love them, too, but if they keep this up, they'll kill every bit of feeling I have for them. Kill it dead."

"Phil's fun," I said.

"He is, he is," she responded enthusiastically. "And good, too. That's what most people don't know. So he's been in some trouble. It's all in the past. Does he have to be punished for it the rest of his life? I don't understand my father and mother. Father DiFalcone is always talking about Christian love and forgiveness. They hang on every word that comes out of his mouth. That's what I can't stand about parents, you know. They're such hypocrites."

"If you laid it all out on the table. . . ." I suggested.

"Don't you think I have?" She was applying the paint

so vigorously that little drops of whiteness were flying through the air, landing in her hair and clothes—and in mine. "You don't know my father. He was born in this country, but you'd never think it to listen to him. He told me if Phil came to the door he'd break every bone in his body. He would, too."

"Oh, Claudia, no," I protested.

"Oh, Claudia, yes," she returned grimly. "Believe me, it's a mess. A first-class mess. It's driving me crazy."

"I wish I could help."

"You are helping. By being nice about Geoff's picking me up."

We spent a couple of hours companionably splattering paint over each other, and then Geoff drove me home. Mom was working, and it was another one of Gram's afternoons at the JINS shelter.

"I'll come in," Geoff said.

"No, not today," I returned quickly. I didn't want Gram to walk in and find him there.

"Why not?"

"I have a lot of homework."

"I won't stay long. It's customary to offer the driver some light refreshment." His tone was airy, but his eyes were serious.

"Not today," I repeated as firmly as I could. "Thanks for the ride." I grasped the door handle. Suddenly his hand reached around me and grasped my forearm. I turned to face him.

"Dinah," he exclaimed sharply, "I think we have to get something straight. I like you a lot." Still grasping my arm, he looked directly into my eyes. "Do you like me, Dinah?" he asked. "I thought you did, but I need to make sure. Do you want us to be friends?"

"Yes, Geoff," I said, "I want us to be friends." I put my hand on top of his and pressed it.

"Then say the real reason I can't come into your house for half an hour. Your grandmother doesn't like me."

I sighed, and nodded. "My mother and my grandfather aren't too crazy about our relationship, either. I'm afraid the only sure friend you have in there is Jonathan."

"What about you, Dinah?"

"Me? Why, of course you have me."

"Then why don't *you* let me come in? If your grandmother finds me, she'll just have to make the best of it. I see what's going on with Phil and Claudia and Mr. and Mrs. Santora. I sure don't want to be part of anything like that."

"Well, of course my family isn't like Claudia's," I protested. "They would never *forbid* me. It's a different case anyway. They haven't got anything against you personally. It's just that you're not Jewish. Being Jewish means a lot to them."

"Who do they think I am?" he asked with a touch of petulance. "The Grand Inquisitor, offering them a choice between conversion and the flames?"

How could I explain? Even I knew that he was, in some way, a threat. "It's complicated," I said.

"When I take you out," he announced firmly, "I'm not going to meet you under a streetlamp someplace."

"No, of course not. And I would never lie about going out with you. They know about the dance. They don't like it, but they're not going to stop me. They can't stop me."

He brushed my cheek with his lips. "I'll call you," he said.

"Yes," I said. "Call me."

I climbed out of the car and made my way slowly up the path, clomping each foot down in front of the other one, as if I were slogging through a frozen swamp. This was going to be tougher than I'd thought.

Gram came home from the JINS shelter half an hour later. I was in the kitchen, peeling potatoes. I usually started supper if I got in before Gram or Mom. Gram left the menu stuck on the refrigerator with a magnet in the shape of a banana.

She started talking before she'd even taken off her hat and coat. "Two new kids today," she said, "two who weren't there last week. But all the kids who were there last week are still there. They're not supposed to stay longer than a month. Some of them have been there six months. There's no other place for them to go. That house is going to burst one of these days. They need to build an addition."

She was so upset about the overcrowding in the JINS shelter that she'd forgotten she wasn't speaking to me. "What's the new kids' problem?" I asked.

"A girl and a boy abused at home. In different ways. So they've become abusive themselves. In different ways." She sank into a chair with a sigh. Her makeup had faded and I could see the circles under her eyes. It was one of the rare occasions when she looked her age. "It's so awful," she said. "Kids, they're just kids."

"Maybe you shouldn't volunteer there if it upsets you so much," I suggested.

"But I love it," she said. "It's terrible to hear their stories when they come in. But some of them are such great kids, in spite of everything that's happened to them. Not all of them, of course, but some of them. And you know the staff, they're super. Some of the kids are really helped. You can see it."

"You help, too, Gram," I said.

She didn't deny it. "I listen," she admitted, "and they need to talk." She was the kind of person to whom strangers in adjoining seats on airplanes spilled out their entire life stories between New York and Chicago. "That's why I can't give it up," she said. "I really feel needed. And it's only two afternoons a week. I guess I can stand it."

I poured a cup of coffee from the pot on the stove and put it down in front of her. She took a deep sip and then looked up at me. "Thank you, Dinah," she said.

"You're welcome, Gram."

"I'm still mad at you, you know."

When Gram had things on her mind, she needed to spill them out. I'd been the only person home, so she'd spilled them out to me.

66

"I'm glad you're talking to me," I said. "I wish you'd also try to understand me. Like you do those kids."

She uttered a grim little laugh. "Those kids have real problems," she said. "All you're doing is messing up a good thing."

"No," I said, "that's what you're doing."

SIX

The decorations for the Student Council Dance were a triumph. Everyone said so. I looked pretty good, too. The first person who told me that was Geoff. After he said it, I didn't need anyone else to say it. But Claire did, and Claudia, and some others. Luckily I had an outfit, the one Mom had just bought me for Jonathan's bar mitzvah.

My mother was more than a little upset when she saw what I had on. "That's for the bar mitzvah," she said. "You should save it. It's too springlike for February anyway."

"February's exactly when you need something that says spring," I retorted. "Besides, I haven't got anything else."

"You have a closet full of clothes."

"Nothing suitable. I haven't been to nine hundred dances in my lifetime."

"Suppose you spill soda on it, or tear it or something?"

"Mom, if I'd asked you, would you have bought me a new dress for this dance?"

She had the grace to look a little sheepish.

"You should forbid her to wear that outfit, Ellen," Gram said. "You should absolutely forbid her."

"Mother, we've been through this," my mother returned sharply.

"Miriam, drop it already," Gramps said.

"I thought you were on my side," Gram said.

"I'm tired of this conversation," Gramps snapped. "She's going—at least let her look pretty and have a good time."

When he picked me up, Geoff didn't come any further into the house than the front hall. I called out, "Good night."

From the family room, Mom and Gramps answered me. "Good night. Have fun." Jonathan was upstairs. Gram said nothing.

"You look super," Geoff said. "Like a cover girl on a magazine."

Claire and Charlie were meeting us at the dance. We returned to Harcourt Avenue for Claudia. Since they were neighbors, it would have made much more sense for Geoff to pick her up first and then come to get me. But he didn't want to do it that way. He wanted to pick me up first. Fortunately, it was a long way up the Santoras' walk. In the dark, they wouldn't notice me waiting in the car.

After that, we went for Phil. A few blocks from his house, Bartine Street was all torn up. A water main had burst or something. We had to detour all the way down to the river and back up Elridge Avenue in order to reach his place.

Phil met us at the curb, resplendent in a white suit and a bright print shirt, like a character on a TV show.

We retraced our way along the detour in order to get back to Harmony Boulevard, the road that would take us to the school. This time Claudia was absolutely firm about not letting Phil kiss her. "I'm not going to arrive at that dance looking like I've just survived a tornado," she said.

Phil had to content himself with putting his arm around her and gazing out the window. "It's years since I've been down here by the river," he said. "I used to come here with my father almost every day in the summer when I was a kid, to fish."

"Catch anything?" Geoff asked.

"Nah. It was just as polluted then as it is now. A fish would need steel gills to survive in that water, but I liked coming. It was the only time my father talked normally to me, instead of shouting out orders. . . . Hey, slow down a minute," he urged suddenly.

Geoff obliged. Phil pointed to a small brick apartment building, a tenement, actually, across the road from the river. "It's empty," he said. "Abandoned."

He was right. The windows of the building were boarded up. The only light came from the streetlamps and the moon. The other structures in the neighborhood weren't dwellings, but rather small machine shops, stores selling auto parts, and similar enterprises—all dark and closed for the night. The street was silent, deserted, abandoned, like the tenement.

Geoff speeded up again. "My father used to live in that building," Phil said. "When I was a kid, that's where he lived. He and a couple of other guys owned it. I guess they still do. I didn't know it was empty."

"Where's your dad living now?" I asked. Maybe it was the wrong question, but I couldn't help being curious, and anyway, he'd raised the subject.

Phil shrugged. "Last I heard, out in Hunterdon County. That was Christmas. He could have moved three times since then for all I know."

"Kids on their own live in buildings like that," Claudia said. "I read an article about it. In big cities, sometimes they take over abandoned apartments."

"Yeah," Phil agreed. "Junkies do that, too."

For a moment, the four of us were silent. I don't know what the others were thinking about. As for me, there I was, all dressed up in my expensive outfit, sitting next to a boy I was crazy about in the comfortable front seat of a BMW, because he'd decided Rent-A-Wreck wasn't good enough for the dance and had borrowed his father's car. I couldn't help comparing myself with those other teenagers, the ones Claudia and Phil were talking about, hanging out in broken-down apartment houses, with no one to care whether they lived or died, except each other—maybe. It was an uncomfortable image.

But then we arrived at the school, and after that I didn't think of anything else. It was perfect, and I was smart enough to relish that, without any thought for what had gone before, or what might come later.

The gym was already crowded when we got there. Jerry Goldfarb, a photographer on our school newspaper, the *Indian*, snapped our picture as the four of us entered the room. That wasn't because of me or Phil or Claudia. It was because of Geoff.

I thought I knew what the place looked like; after all, I'd been in school until six o'clock finishing up the decorations. But now I was both surprised and satisfied. Full of people, with the lights low, it had turned into the glowing magic garden I'd imagined at that very first committee meeting. We called the dance "A Very Early Spring." I'd painted a banner for the wall inscribed with that legend and emblazoned with a somewhat primitive but not ineffective enlargement of van Gogh's famous painting of sunflowers in a vase.

The disk jockeys hired by the Student Council had set up their equipment under one of the basketball backboards. The room was filled to the furthest corner with the rich, dreamy sound of mellow saxophones and muted trumpets. Without a word, I moved into Geoff's arms and we began to dance. It seemed to me that I had wings on my heels.

We drank soda and joked around a little with the others between numbers. But mostly we danced. I wasn't interested in talking. I was interested only in feeling what I was feeling. It was the same for him. He didn't have to say so. I could tell. He whispered in my ear, "Happy spring." I wanted the moment to last forever.

I wasn't the only one. None of us really wanted the evening to end. The six of us went back to Claire's house, consumed plates full of nachos as fast as Claire could prepare them, drank cases of soda, and played an utterly hysterical game of Trivial Pursuit, the guys against the girls. The guys cheated, but the girls won anyway.

It was almost three in the morning when Phil, Claudia,

Geoff, and I left Claire's. At Phil's, I waited in the car with Geoff while Phil and Claudia did whatever it was they did inside the dark, silent little house. Geoff opened the glove compartment and pulled out a package. "I bought you a present."

"But, Geoff, why?"

"Just because I wanted to. A memento I guess, so you won't forget this evening."

As if I ever could. "Oh, Geoff, I feel terrible. I didn't get you a thing."

"Why should you? Don't get too excited," he added diffidently. "It's nothing much."

I undid the paper and opened the box. Inside was a blue Smurf. He was quite large for a Smurf, maybe four inches high, and dressed in white trousers and a white pointy cap. A bashful smile graced his face, and in his outstretched hand he carried a bunch of yellow flowers, as if he were presenting them to the queen of England. "Geoff, he's adorable," I cried. "He's the cutest thing." I ran the tip of my finger over the bouquet. "What kind of flowers do you think he's carrying?"

"Whatever kind of flowers you want them to be."

"I think they're daffodils. Golden daffodils. I love him." I lifted him to my face and touched the top of his head with my lips.

"What a waste," Geoff said. He put his arms around me and kissed me, a long delicious kiss. The Smurf dropped out of my hand. I didn't see or hear Claudia come back to the car, and neither did Geoff. She startled us by tapping on the window, and we broke apart. I blushed, and she grinned.

"Listen, guys," she said, as she opened the door, "I hate to break this up, but I have to get home. I'm an hour past my curfew as it is."

"Whose fault is that?" Geoff said with a touch of grumpiness.

She curled herself up in a corner of the backseat. Her grin had disappeared; she was frowning and her eyes looked tired. "I'm sick of this," she said. "A few kisses in the back of your car, a fast good night in Phil's living room. It's no way to live."

"Claudia," Geoff said, "what can you do about it?"

"Maybe we should run away. Maybe get married."

"Oh, no!" I exclaimed. "Don't do that."

"Why not?" Her tone was sharp.

"You're too young."

"Who's in love, except young people? And my parents won't let us be together." There was a bleakness in her eyes that I'd never seen before.

"What would you live on?" I asked.

"We could get jobs."

Geoff shook his head. "Oh, Claudia, what do you and Phil know how to do? You can't live on what he makes sweeping up a carpet store. Not if you have to pay rent and all that stuff. You don't even have a car to run away in."

"Phil could get a car."

"The same way he got Dr. MacPherson's Porsche? The police would catch up with you in two days. In two hours."

I turned and faced her. "It's a better idea to work on your family," I said. "You have more chance of succeeding at that than at running away together. I mean—Claudia, if you got married at seventeen you could ruin your life."

She uncurled herself and leaned forward. Her face was so close to mine I could see sparks in her clear hazel eyes. "What do you know about my family?" she cried. "You, with your nice understanding mother who lets you do whatever you want. You don't know what goes on in my house. So don't give me any advice." She tapped Geoff on the shoulder. "That goes for you, too, wise guy."

Shaken, I pulled back. But I didn't turn away. "I'm sorry," I said. "I didn't mean to sound like a prig. But, listen, if you can't talk to your folks, talk to someone else."

"Like who?" She leaned back again in her seat.

"Maybe Father DiFalcone," Geoff suggested.

"Don't be ridiculous. Father DiFalcone thinks cold showers, vigorous exercise, and ten Hail Marys can cure anything."

"Your guidance counselor?" I queried, feeling almost silly.

"Miss Van Nostrand? She hasn't said two words to me since I got into high school. I make up my program, she signs it. She's never done one single thing to suggest she's the kind of person I could talk to."

"There must be someone," I said. "Some other relative. A family friend. The school psychologist. Someone."

We pulled up in front of Claudia's house. Geoff got out of the car to walk in with her. "Well, it was a nice evening," she commented. "For a while. But then Phil and I had to go and get depressed."

"Don't do anything crazy, Claudia," I said. "Okay?"

She didn't reply, but she smiled a little. She wasn't mad at me. Claudia's fits of temper came and went like spring showers.

But her gloom had effectively killed the euphoria which earlier had surrounded Geoff and me like a cloud. "Parents have all these rules that really don't matter," Geoff said. "It's like they don't know what's important. And so they end up getting exactly what they're trying to avoid."

"What do you mean?"

"The last thing the Santoras want is for Claudia and Phil to run away or elope or something like that. Yet they might drive them into doing just that."

Actually, I could see why Mr. and Mrs. Santora didn't like Phil. Geoff could, too. He'd admitted as much the night we'd gone bowling. Geoff suspected that if Phil wanted a car, he might not hesitate to just take one. What were Mr. and Mrs. Santora supposed to do? Say, "Sure, Claudia, go out with a thief, it's okay with us?"

Only Phil was other things, too—funny, generous, a friend. He was like the evening had been: complicated. But then wasn't everyone? Wasn't everything?

At my front door, Geoff kissed me briefly and left. In the family room, I dug Gram's flower dictionary out of her work bag, where she stored it along with the tablecloth and the embroidery silks. I flipped the pages until I came to the

D's. *Daffodil* was the first flower on the page. It meant "regard." That wasn't quite "love." "Love" would have been a rose. But it was pretty good for a first step. Of course, Geoff didn't know what daffodils were supposed to mean. He hadn't even known the flowers in the Smurf's hand *were* daffodils.

I went upstairs to my room. I took my Smurf out of his little box and set him on my dresser with the dolls my mother had brought back for me from her trips and the Eskimo mask some cousins from Montreal had given me. I put the Smurf in front. He wasn't the most valuable object up there, but he was by far the most precious. And then I went to sleep.

Over the next week, I saw Geoff daily at school. We spoke on the phone most nights. In the hall sometimes I passed Claudia and Phil, their arms around each other, their faces grave. They said hello, but absently, their minds obviously in some other place.

At home, we were closing in on Jonathan's bar mitzvah. Each day when we got back from school, Jonathan and I ran for the pile of mail in the basket on the table in the hall, to check on who'd responded to the invitations. Mom and Gram discussed the seating. Actually, discussed is too mild a term. What they did is fight. A couple of times Gramps, fearing blows, came between them. Almost every night, Jonathan practiced chanting his *haftarah* or some other part of the service for us. He and Gramps were working on his speech. Gramps was a good writer. When he sent a letter to a newspaper, even to the *New York Times*, it usually got published.

Thursday afternoon Geoff drove Claire and me to my house so we could study together for the English test we had the next day. It was on *Julius Caesar*, and Mrs. Theobald had warned us that it would be full of quotations to identify, so Claire and I had decided to spend an hour throwing lines at each other. "You'll stay for dinner," I suggested to Claire, on the way home.

75

"Sure," Claire agreed. "Why not? I remember your bar mitzvah," she added, licking her lips. "The stuff they served at the reception was delicious. Especially the hors d'oeuvres. Will they have them at Jonathan's reception?"

"They're standard fare at Jewish parties."

"You ought to invite me, so I can eat them again."

I laughed. "It could be arranged, I think." At least twenty people had declined for one reason or another. There was room for replacements, and I thought that if I mentioned Claire's desire to be among them, an invitation would be forthcoming.

"I'd like to come, too," Geoff said.

We'd talked about Jonathan's bar mitzvah before. I remembered.

"I don't recall any wonderful hors d'oeuvres at the bar mitzvahs I went to when I was in seventh grade. This is your chance to fill a big hole in my life." He was driving and could give me no more than a brief glance. But I saw the question in his eyes.

I swallowed hard. "I don't issue the invitations. But I'll ask. About both of you." It might work if I mentioned the two of them at the same time. Geoff could perhaps slip past along with Claire. My family adored Claire.

Later that evening, after supper, Claire's dad came to pick her up. After I'd shut the door behind her, I walked into the family room where Mom, Gram, and Gramps were watching TV, more or less. Gram was also embroidering a mimosa branch, Gramps was reading the paper, and Mom was sitting at the table writing checks. "Claire would like to come to Jonathan's bar mitzvah," I announced.

Gramps lowered the sound on the TV. "Why not?" he said. "We should have thought of it ourselves. She's practically a member of the family."

"Of course she can come," Mom agreed. "We have the room."

"And Geoff wants to come, too," I added casually.

Gramps snapped the TV off entirely.

Gram said, "Over my dead body."

Mom said, "I don't think that's a good idea, Dinah."

I felt the heat of anger rise in me, and I struggled to keep it out of my voice. "Why is it all right for Claire to come and not Geoff?"

"You know why," Gram said.

"No, Gram." I turned and faced her. "I don't know. She's no more Jewish than he is."

"Claire is a girl," Gram said. "Geoff is a boy."

"So?"

"Dinah," Mom said, "sit down. Let's talk about this."

"All right." I pulled a straight-backed chair away from the table and plopped myself into it. "I'd like to hear how you're going to justify this one. Are you going to start by telling me that Claire is different because I'll never marry Claire, but I might marry Geoff? Are you going to try to tell me that Jewish survival is endangered if Geoff comes to Jonathan's bar mitzvah?"

"Dinah!" Gramps's voice was unusually sharp. "Your mother and grandmother can speak for themselves. You don't have to put words in their mouths."

"Now listen, Dinah." My mother's voice was the epitome of sweet reason. She'd used the very same tone on us all our lives. "Dinah, I wish I could let you eat the leftover chocolate cake for breakfast, but I can't. It'll give you a stomachache now and bad skin when you're older. I wish I could let Jonathan go over to Howard's to watch *The Curse of the Living Dead*, but I can't. You know how prone he is to nightmares."

I folded my arms across my chest. "I'm listening."

The tablecloth lay untouched in Gram's lap, as she fixed her eyes on my mother and me. But she said nothing, apparently having decided, for once, not to interfere. I didn't know whether that was a good sign or a bad one.

"You know we don't approve of the fact that you're going out with this boy," my mother began, rather formally, as if she were laying out a business plan.

"Just because he isn't Jewish." The words burst out of me.

Gram pursed her lips together.

"We have nothing against Geoff Ruggles personally," Gramps interjected. "He seems to be a very fine young man."

"You know how we feel," my mother said. "You know our reasons. You choose to go out with him anyway. You're almost sixteen; we can't stop you. We're not going to lock you in your room. We're not going to cut off your allowance. Such measures are ridiculous, and counterproductive, as a rule." The voice of sweet reason disappeared. Suddenly she was speaking loudly and sharply. "But it's *I* who am issuing invitations to Jonathan's bar mitzvah. They go out over *my* name. And no one's going to be at that bar mitzvah whom I don't want at that bar mitzvah!"

My shock was so great that for a moment it was all I could feel. Such an ultimatum was not something I'd ever expected to hear come out of my mother's mouth. I didn't give her a chance to say any more.

"You're a hypocrite, Mother," I cried. I turned to my grandparents. "And you, too. You're hypocrites. You work for the American Civil Liberties Union. You write letters to the editor about the dangers of prejudice and intolerance. 'Pick your friends because you share interests, because they're good people, not because of their race, color, or creed.' That's what you always told me. Well, it was nonsense, wasn't it? You never believed it. Not for a minute. What you meant is, 'You can have any friends you want—so long as they're people like us.' "

"That's unfair, Dinah," Gramps protested. "Look at Claire. We never said a word about her and you know it. We love her. Geoff is different, that's all."

"There's no difference," I shot back. "Geoff is my friend. He just happens to be a boy, that's all. Hypocrites. The three of you."

I stood up and marched out of the room, my back straight, my chin up. But once I was out of their sight, I rushed up the stairs, ran into my room, slammed my door, and threw myself down on the bed. I cried and cried, drowning in self-pity. What hurt the most was that somewhere inside of me I knew what my family meant. Geoff *was* different from Claire. He wasn't just a friend, the way that she was, or that Josie and Brenda were. I knew that as well as Gramps did.

I'd never been so confused in my life. I buried my head under the pillow, like an ostrich in the sand.

But when it came, I heard the knock on the door. "Don't come in," I cried.

"It's Mother."

"Don't come in!"

"Please, Dinah. I have something to tell you."

I turned over and blew my nose. "I don't want to hear it."

"It's about me, not about you." There was a pause. When she spoke again, it was almost in a whisper. "It's very interesting."

I sat up and let my feet hang over the edge of the bed. "Oh, all right. It isn't locked." She opened the door slowly and stepped into the room. "This better be good," I warned.

She leaned down and kissed me on the top of the head. "I'm sorry you're so unhappy," she said. "Really, I am."

"No, you're not."

"Don't tell me how I feel, Dinah." She sat down next to me. "I *am* sorry. You don't believe that, but I am."

"I thought we weren't going to talk about me."

"We won't talk about you." She ran her fingers through her hair and for a moment rested her head against her palm. "There's someone else who wants to come to Jonathan's bar mitzvah."

"Someone else you won't invite?"

"Yes. A friend of mine. A male friend."

"Sam Midman came to my bat mitzvah," I said. "Of course, you couldn't have him at Jonathan's. He's probably going out with someone else by now."

"I heard he's getting married. I'm not talking about Sam Midman. Sam Midman doesn't mean beans in my life."

"But, Mom, you dated him for three years!"

She shrugged. "He's a nice guy. You have to go out with somebody. No, the man I'm talking about is not being invited to Jonathan's bar mitzvah for the same reason I don't want to invite Geoff—he's not Jewish."

I put my hand on her arm. "Who are you talking about?"

She blushed, the way that I blush. I'd never seen her do that before. "Elliot," she said. "Elliot Chickering."

My hands struck each other with a sharp clap. Chicken Little. Of course. Jonathan had been right; I had been wrong. "Does Gram know?" I asked softly.

She shook her head.

"Gramps?"

"I think he guesses. Like Jonathan."

"Boy, the ladies in your house are blind as bats, aren't they?"

"There hasn't been anything to see, Dinah. That's the point. There hasn't been anything. I wouldn't let it happen."

But there had been something. A kiss, at least. "Because he's not Jewish," I said.

She nodded. "I won't start what I can't finish. I like Elliot a lot. I know if I went out with him, the way he wants me to, I might fall in love with him. So I won't go. I keep my distance. That way I avoid hurting him, and hurting myself, too."

I thought she was fooling herself. I thought she was in love with him already.

She was still speaking. "I won't even let him come to Jonathan's bar mitzvah. No one would say a word if he came, not even Gram. He's my boss; it would be perfectly logical for me to invite him. But I won't. I'm not going to give him any encouragement, that's all."

"But, Mom, that's terrible!" I cried. "You're breaking your heart and his, too, for what? It's the silliest thing I ever heard."

"Dinah, listen to me." She put her hands on my shoulders. "No one's heart is being broken. It hasn't gone that far, and it never will. But I'll tell you this much. He's never been married. If he had a wife, he'd want a child. At least one. If we fell in love, if we got married, if we had a child, how would we bring that child up? I'd want it to be Jewish; he'd want it to be Christian. What would we do? Who would that child be?"

"But, Mom, that's so far down the road. . . ."

"I guess that's the difference between a kid and an adult," my mother replied quietly. "An adult looks down the road; a kid doesn't."

I sniffled and brushed at my eyes with the back of my hand.

Mom smiled. "Don't cry for me, baby," she said. "I'm *not* in love with Mr. Chickering. That's the point. I won't let myself be."

But I did feel sorry for her. My heart ached for her. There was only one thing sadder that I knew about her. She had loved my father, and he had died. That had been a terrible waste. This was a different kind of waste, but a waste, nevertheless. Or so it seemed to me.

SEVEN

"Will a sports jacket do?" Geoff asked. He sat down next to me, offering me the carton of popcorn he'd just purchased. We were at one of the narrow, dumpy multi-cinemas in the shopping mall, waiting for the movie to begin.

"Do for what?" I asked.

"For Jonathan's bar mitzvah."

Coward that I was, up until that minute, I hadn't told him. I took a deep breath, and then made my voice sound as casual as I could. "Don't worry about it. You aren't coming."

He did not respond casually. He stared at me, frowning. "What do you mean?"

I didn't have any words to say that were different from the ones I'd said already. I clenched my clammy fists, urged my stomach to settle down, and blessed the half-light in which the auditorium was cast. I didn't want him to see how nervous this conversation was making me. I took another deep breath and plunged in.

"You know how my family feels about my dating someone who isn't Jewish. They can't stop me from doing that, but they can show their disapproval by not allowing you to come to the bar mitzvah."

Though I couldn't look at him, I could feel his eyes still fixed on my face. "So what did you say?" he asked.

"I screamed and yelled, of course. But what could I do? It's not my party. I'm not issuing the invitations. My mother is. If she says no, then it's no."

"What would they have done if you'd said you wouldn't go unless I came too?"

Now it was my turn to stare at him. "You want me to blackmail them?"

"Dinah," he said, "the whole thing seems so ridiculous to me. My parents don't object to the fact that we go together. Why should yours?"

"You know, Geoff," I replied quietly, "this problem is bigger than just you and me. Hitler's goal was to wipe the Jews from the face of the earth. He almost succeeded. Six million Jews were killed. It's something we can't forget. Maybe that makes us paranoid, but that's how it is. My folks see interdating as a threat to Jewish survival. It makes them very nervous. It has nothing to do with you personally." How many times had I said that? Yet how could he not take it personally?

"Our dating is a threat to Jewish survival?" He shook his head in utter disbelief.

"That's how *they* see it," I returned. "I'm not talking about me." I put my hand on his arm. "I explained all this to you before. I don't see why I have to go through it again."

"I didn't understand then, and I don't understand now."

The theater darkened and the music came up. I was never so glad to see a picture begin since I'd started going to the movies. I knew this conversation wasn't over; if I had some more time, maybe I could gather my resources. Maybe a light bulb would turn on in my head and suddenly I'd stumble on the words to make him understand. It wasn't likely, but it wasn't impossible either. "We'll talk about it later," I said.

He didn't reply. We sat silently through the movie. He didn't take my hand; he didn't put his arm around me. He didn't even make any jokes about what was happening on the screen. And I didn't come up with any bright ideas.

Afterward, as we were leaving the theater, I said, "You blame me, don't you? You think it's my fault, that I didn't try hard enough to persuade them."

"I know you care a lot for them," he said.

I nodded.

"I presume they care for you."

"Yes, they do."

"Then if it's something you want very much, and it costs them nothing to let you have it, how can they deny you?"

"It does cost them," I said. "That's the point. It does."

But that was the very thing he couldn't grasp. For a fleeting moment I was jealous of Claudia. Her folks disapproved of Phil, but she was totally on Phil's side. I had a different problem—ambivalence was tearing me apart.

We approached the car. "I'm not very hungry," Geoff said. "Are you?"

"No. All that popcorn." I'd scarcely eaten two handfuls.

We had little to say to each other on the ride home. He pulled into the driveway. Before I climbed out of the car, I spoke to him. "Listen, Geoff, we have to talk some more about this." I didn't know what I could say. But I also knew I couldn't leave it like this, a darkness as black as a hole in the sky stretching between us.

"I guess so," he replied. "But not tonight. I'm tired."

"All right." I opened the door. "You don't have to see me in. Good night."

"Good night, Dinah."

I lay awake in bed for a long time, alternately shivering and sweating. I was afraid. This could be the end for Geoff and me. We'd barely begun, and maybe now it was over. If it was, that was Gram's fault and Mom's and even Gramps's. But I realized I wasn't angry at my family alone. I was mad at Gram and Gramps and Mom. But I was mad at Geoff, too. He thought if I really cared for him, I'd have fought my folks harder. I thought if he really cared for me, what my folks said or did wouldn't matter so much.

Tossing and turning in bed was getting me no place. I sat up, switched on the light, got out of bed, and found my history text on my desk. It was the dullest book I could think of. I lay down again and began to read. After a while, my head nodded and my lids grew heavy. Without being quite aware of it, I fell asleep. In the morning, when I woke, I saw that the book had tumbled on the floor and that the lamp was still on. I reached to snap it off and glanced at the clock. My head ached and my mouth was dry, as if I hadn't slept at all. But it was ten-thirty. I was glad. That meant there was less of the day to get through.

I did homework. I read the paper. I baked for the Friday night of the bar mitzvah weekend and put the almond cookies and nut cakes I made in the freezer. I sewed on buttons and stitched torn seams, depleting a pile of mending that had been growing in one of my drawers for six months. I held up my end of two lengthy conversations with Claire. But all that activity was nothing more than whistling in the dark. Each time the phone rang, I dropped everything and rushed to answer it. It was never Geoff. Of course, I could have called him. But I didn't.

Monday I went to school with my heart in my throat. Were we still a couple or were we not? We would have to talk. I'd know for sure in a little while, one way or the other. It would be better than wondering.

I was hanging my coat in my locker when I saw Claudia rushing down the hall, her mouth grim, her eyes looking neither to the right nor the left. She was alone.

I moved into her path. "Slow down, Claudia!" I exclaimed. "You'll run someone over. What's the matter?"

She stopped and stared at me blankly. For a moment it appeared as if she didn't know who I was. Then her pupils seemed to focus. "Dinah!" she cried, as she opened her purse and withdrew a copy of the Lenape High *Indian*. "Did you see this? Did you see it?"

I pulled her over to the side, next to my locker. "Yes, of course," I said. The *Indian* came out the fourth Friday of every month, full of stale news in which no one was any longer interested. The issue that had been distributed in homeroom the previous Friday morning had contained a full page of photos from the Student Council Dance. "The four of us look pretty good, don't we?"

I hadn't thought about the picture Jerry Goldfarb had snapped as we'd walked into the dance until I'd noticed our four shining faces in the paper, bright with anticipation. Geoff had remarked that Jerry was a terrific photographer. "I'm going to ask him to make a couple of copies for us," he'd said. Now I wondered if Geoff was going to bother. Well, if he didn't, I would. It would be a memento. That and the Smurf.

Claudia was shouting. "Pretty good? You think we look pretty good? Oh, my God!" She put her face in her hands and her shoulders shook.

"What's the matter?"

She lifted her head and dropped her arms to her sides. She seemed to be laughing grimly and crying all at once. "My parents saw that picture."

"How perfectly terrible. How did it happen?" I'd known that sooner or later her parents had to find out, but this was not the moment to remind her of that fact.

"I brought the *Indian* home in my notebook. I didn't think anything of it." She shook her head, as if amazed at her own stupidity. "I put the notebook on the kitchen table. My mother noticed the newspaper sticking out, and she said, 'Oh, let me see it. I like to know what's going on.' It wasn't until that moment I realized she mustn't get her hands on it. But it was too late. She'd already grabbed it. Right off, she noticed the picture."

"Did you invent some kind of excuse?"

Claudia nodded. "I tried to make her believe Phil was your date and Geoff was mine. I said we'd just gotten mixed up walking into the gym. She didn't buy it for one second. She screamed and yelled. 'You lied to me. You've done nothing but lie to me for six months.' She slapped my face. Oh, Dinah, it was awful. I ran upstairs and hid myself in my room. What else could I do?"

"Nothing."

"Then my father came home." She shivered, and folded her arms across her chest, holding on to herself as tightly as she could. "I didn't think things could get worse, but they did. I'm surprised the neighbors didn't come knocking at the door, wondering what in the name of heaven was going on. I'll spare you the gory details. In the end what they did was lock me up. I'm not to go out of the house except to go to school for the rest of the year. If Phil comes around, they'll call the cops. Geoff can't come, either. That's because he was part of the lie. As a matter of fact, none of my friends can visit me, because I'm untrustworthy and immoral." She choked on the words as she spoke them. "They're acting like I'm some kind of criminal. And I don't know what to do about it. I'm going to find that Jerry Goldfarb and ream him out. Ruby Swartout, too." Ruby was the editor-in-chief of the *Indian*.

"It's not their fault. How could they know that picture was going to get you into so much trouble?"

"Everyone knows my parents hate Phil."

"No, they don't," I insisted. "It's the biggest problem in the world to you, so you think everyone's aware of it. But most of the time other people don't know what's going on inside of you. Just one or two close friends—if that."

She leaned against my locker, her shoulders sagging. For a moment, she looked like a lost little girl. "Oh, you're right. I know you're right. I'm going crazy, that's all. I have to blame someone."

"What does Phil say?"

"Well, the thing is, I haven't spoken to him. They took the phone out of my room, and they won't let me answer any of the other extensions when they ring. Phil never calls me at home anyway. I call him, and then only when no one's watching. Believe me, this weekend I was watched every second. For some reason, Phil isn't in school this morning. I was waiting for him to get off his bus. When he didn't, I was so disappointed I cried."

"Come on," I said soothingly. "Let's go to the public phone by the main office. You can call him from there."

She actually smiled. "Boy, am I a wreck. I never even thought of that."

The bell rang while she was in the telephone booth, and I had to hurry to homeroom. I didn't see her for the rest of the day. It occurred to me that she might have left the building.

In the art room I had a few minutes before class began to talk to Geoff. Bad as I felt about what had happened to Claudia and Phil, I was glad I had some reason other than our own problem to approach him. "Did you hear about Claudia?" I asked.

"No. What happened?"

"Her parents found out." I described what I knew of recent events in the Santora household.

He banged his fist into his open palm. "I knew they'd find out sooner or later. She should have called me. I would have gone over."

"They won't let her use the phone. Anyway, you're not welcome in that house any more than Phil, because you were part of the lie."

"Persona non grata everywhere," he said. "I'm beginning to wonder if there's something even my best friend won't tell me."

I frowned. "What do you mean?"

"You know. I can't go to her house. I can't go to your house."

"You can come to my house," I protested. "You can call me up. My folks are nothing like Claudia's. They haven't put me in jail."

"I don't see much difference," Geoff said, with perfect calm. "Maybe they're not as blatant, but the effect is the same. They're prejudiced and narrow-minded." He said it out loud, just like that. "Prejudiced and narrow-minded." He might just as well have called them liars and thieves. "You know, you've said a hundred times they have nothing against me personally. But they do, you know. The

Santoras think Phil isn't good enough for Claudia, and your family thinks I'm not good enough for you!"

I felt my face grow hot. "Geoff!" I cried. "How dare you!"

He didn't raise his voice, but the tension in it was palpable. It grated on my ears like sandpaper. "It's true. They don't think Christians are good enough for Jews."

"You know, Geoff, how would your parents feel if you married a girl who wouldn't put up a Christmas tree in the living room? They wouldn't like it so much. But *I* wouldn't take that personally."

"Don't worry," he returned icily. "It won't happen."

That was the worst thing he'd said so far. I knew his feelings were badly hurt. But now, so were mine. "My folks aren't what you think they are," I insisted. "They're not. You just don't understand."

He shrugged. "Maybe not."

"Take your seats," Mr. Wolleck called. "It's time to get started."

My eyes fell. "Well, Geoff," I said, "I guess I'll—I guess I'll see you around."

He nodded. Blinking hard, I turned away and almost ran to my easel. It was all over, and so quickly, too. I'd had no chance to really explain. But what was there to say, really, that I hadn't said already? How could I make him understand in ten minutes things about my family that had taken me a lifetime to learn?

I opened my box of coals and went to work. I wasn't going to let Geoff see me cry. I wasn't going to let anyone see me cry. I put one foot in front of the other and somehow got through to the end of the day.

At dinner, I told my family.

"Geoff and I broke up," I announced.

"That's good," Gram said.

"It's terrible," I cried. "I feel sick about it."

"Then why did you do it?" Gramps wanted to know.

"I didn't exactly do it," I admitted. "It just sort of happened. Because of you! We broke up because he thinks you're prejudiced and narrow-minded. I can't let him say things like that about you. If he thinks that about you, he thinks that about me, too."

"If he really liked you so much, don't you think he would have been more understanding?" Mom asked.

Like Mr. Chickering? Willing to hang out on the fringes of Mom's life, year after year after year? No, Geoff wasn't any Elliot Chickering. The way Geoff saw it, I was the one who didn't understand him.

"Mom, that's not how it is," I said. "You don't understand, either."

"I'm trying to understand," she said. "Let's talk about it."

"Not now. Not ever!" I left them and climbed up the stairs to my own room. What was the point of talking? Geoff didn't understand them, they didn't understand him, none of them understood me. We could jabber away for a year and not change that. As a method of communication, talking stunk. Unfortunately, there was no other.

One person I had to talk to, right away, was Claudia. She and I could understand each other all right. I needed to find out what had happened when she'd phoned Phil, and I also needed to make sure she was okay.

I looked her number up in the book and dialed it. A man I presumed to be her father answered. "May I please speak to Claudia," I said.

"Who is this?" He sounded like a prosecuting attorney.

"It's Dinah Adler, a friend of hers."

"I never heard of you, Dinah Adler," he returned suspiciously.

Good. That meant he hadn't bothered to read the caption under the picture in the *Indian*. "I'm sort of a new friend," I said.

"Claudia isn't feeling well." Why didn't he just say she'd been grounded? Why did he bother lying? Did he suppose Claudia hadn't told her friends what had really happened? "She can't come to the phone."

"Will you tell her I called, then? Just to make sure she's all right."

"She's all right. She'll be in school tomorrow."

"Oh, good." I was pretty sure he wouldn't tell her that I'd called. But maybe she'd overheard his end of the conversation. It might make her feel a little better to know someone was thinking of her.

I did my homework. My mother came in and tried to talk, but the conversation fizzled out, mostly because I answered her in monosyllables. I went to bed fairly early. In spite of everything, I fell asleep almost immediately, from simple exhaustion. Nothing knocks a person out like a lot of emotions piled up on top of each other.

The next day in school I saw Geoff in art class. We didn't speak. I wondered if everyone in the school already knew it was off, the way they'd known as soon as it was on. A February romance, come and gone in the shortest month of the year. In biology we'd learned about the life cycle of common houseflies. They emerged from their pupae, mated, laid their eggs, and died in thirty summer days. I felt like a housefly.

Toward the end of the day, a mimeographed absentee list was sent around to all the teachers so they could check to see if any of the kids not present in their classes had actually been cutting. In seventh period, I asked Mr. Nydecker if I could look at his. He handed it to me, and I quickly glanced down the columns. Claudia and Phil were both listed as absent. They hadn't been in school all day.

I took the bus home with Claire and Erna. Claire, of course, knew all about what had happened between Geoff and me. Erna, of course, knew nothing. The news that Geoff and I had broken up might be fairly common knowledge among the upper classes, but it would take some time to reach Erna's ninth-grade ears.

"Gee," Erna said, "I haven't seen you on the bus in ages." She hadn't ridden the bus home herself the day before, so she'd missed my inglorious return to that least desirable mode of transportation. "How come Geoff didn't drive you home today, the way he usually does?" she wondered.

91

"Shut up, Erna," Claire said. "That's not something Dinah wants to talk about."

"Geoff and I are through," I said. "And Claire is right. I don't want to talk about it."

"But you were so perfect together," Erna said.

"We were?" I snapped. "How do you know?"

"I could see it," she said softly. "In your faces."

"Look," I said, "we weren't perfect together. We didn't see eye to eye on a lot of things. You know my family—they care about being Jewish. Actually, it means a lot to me, too. Geoff thought they were positively prehistoric because they wouldn't let my non-Jewish boyfriend come to Jonathan's bar mitzvah, and he didn't make any secret of the way he felt."

"I'm not Jewish," Erna said. "They're letting me come."

"What!" I exclaimed. I didn't remember seeing Erna's name on the list or addressing an envelope to her. The day before, I'd sent one to Claire. She was my dearest friend, and she'd known Jonathan since he was two. She deserved to be at his bar mitzvah. But what possible reason could anyone have for inviting Erna?

"Your grandmother said I could come. She said you all would love to have me."

"Did she? How sweet," I muttered.

"I told her it sounded like a great occasion, and she said it was and I should be there and see for myself. She said she's going to mail me an invitation, so my mom will know it's official."

"You have to bring a present," I said. "A nice present."

"Of course." She frowned. "Dinah, do you think I'm dumb or something?"

I sighed. "No, Erna. You're not dumb. I'm beginning to think you're remarkably clever."

I confronted Gram at dinnertime. But I went through Jonathan.

"You know who Gram invited to your bar mitzvah?" I asked him.

"I invited a lot of people to Jonathan's bar mitzvah,"

Gram said. "That is, your mother invited them, but I asked her to."

Immediately I turned on Gram. "Did you tell her you went and invited Erna? I bet you didn't. I bet you just did it, all on your own."

"Of course she told me," Mom said. "Why should I object?"

"The caterer is charging forty-five dollars a person. I think that's a lot of money to pay just so Erna can satisfy her curiosity."

"Oh, let her come," Jonathan said. "It's all right."

Now I directed my fury at him. "It's all right for Erna to come and not all right for Geoff to come? Honestly, Jonathan, I don't understand you. You're as bad as the rest of them."

Jonathan drew back, his face creased in a hurt frown. "I would like Geoff to come, too," he said. "It wasn't my idea that he shouldn't."

"We've been through that," Gram said. "It's settled."

"You're right," I said. "It's settled. It's all over between Geoff and me, thanks to you. I hope you're happy."

"No one is happy to see you unhappy," Gramps said.

"You know," Jonathan said, "I think this whole affair is causing more trouble than it's worth. You can run away and get married. Too bad you can't run away and get bar mitzvahed."

Mom, Gram, and Gramps laughed. Even I smiled. "All right, all right," I said. "Just don't seat me at the same table with Erna. Promise me that much."

"Well, where's she going to sit, if not with the young people—the older young people?" Gram queried.

"Let her sit with the younger young people." That meant Jonathan's friends. "She's only fourteen—just a year older than most of them."

"That's okay," Jonathan said.

"You're so cooperative." Gram was talking to Jonathan while glaring at me. "It's a pleasure to work with you."

93

"Why should I cooperate with you?" I flung the words at her. "Have you cooperated with me?"

"If Geoff Ruggles can't understand how we feel, you're well rid of him," Gram snapped.

"You know what he thinks?" I addressed the table at large. "He thinks you think gentiles are not good enough for Jews. He thinks that's why you object so much to our dating."

"That," my mother announced, "is the point of view of a narrow-minded person!"

Geoff had called them narrow-minded. Now they were calling him narrow-minded. Next thing you knew, they'd be accusing him of anti-Semitism. I was getting angrier and angrier, not just at them, but at Geoff, too. Only they happened to be there and he wasn't.

"Well, what is the reason, then?" I shouted. "The *real* reason?"

"We told you the real reason," Gram yelled back. "A hundred times."

Jonathan put his hands over his ears and ran from the table. I think Gramps would have done the same thing if he'd had the guts. I wasn't fond of confrontations, either, but I'd been boiling for days now. So had Gram. An eruption was inevitable.

"Gram," I cried, "if you start in on the survival of the Jewish people one more time I will split your head open."

"You don't mean that," my mother said. She didn't yell. She never yelled.

"It's just a metaphor," Gramps suggested.

But Gram and I were beyond the reach of reason. "Why are we living here in Lenape?" I exclaimed. "Why do we belong to a Conservative temple? If you didn't want me and Jonathan to be friends with Christians, why aren't we Hasidim in Crown Heights, never even seeing a non-Jew, except on the subway?"

"You're talking nonsense," Gram said.

"No, I'm not," I insisted. "I'll tell you why we don't live in the modern equivalent of a medieval ghetto. Because you didn't want to give up television and the theater and football games and John Updike novels and the whole wide world. Because *you* didn't want to pay the price." With my fist I struck my chest. "But I—*I* should pay it." I stood up. "Gram, you're a hypocrite. You're a raving hypocrite." I'd accused her of hypocrisy before, but now I was screaming the word in her face. "Hypocrite. Hypocrite."

She stood up, too. She reached out her open palm and slapped my face, hard. I can remember only one other time that she struck me, when I was four and had run into the road. I covered my stinging cheek with my hand.

"Oh, Mother!" my mother exclaimed.

"And you're no better!" I shouted at her.

"Dinah, please. . . ."

"Forget it," I said. "Just forget it. I hate you all."

"Dinah, you don't mean that. . . ."

One part of me was watching the other part of me behave like a two-year-old. Of course I didn't hate them. Not all the time. Mostly I loved them. But I hated them then.

"What are you going to do, Mother?" I asked. "Wash my mouth out with soap?"

"Do you want me to invite Geoff to the bar mitzvah, Dinah? Is that what you want?" my mother asked, her hands grasping the edge of the table.

Now it was my grandmother's turn to utter a word of admonition. "Ellen, no!"

I sank into my seat and leaned back for a moment. The three of them were staring at me—Gramps and Mom with stricken eyes, Gram's shooting arrows. I straightened my shoulders and pushed my spine against the chair rungs.

"No," I said. "Don't invite him. It's too late for that. But I'll never forget this. Never."

"You're heartbroken," Gramps said. "That's why you've talked so crazy tonight."

I tossed my head in Gram's direction. "What's her excuse?"

"Dinah," my mother said very quietly, "go up to your

room. Come back down when you're in better control of yourself. Come back down when you're prepared to apologize—not for your feelings, to which you're entitled, but for the way in which you've wounded the feelings of the people who love you. Especially your grandmother."

I had wounded *her* feelings? Hadn't she wounded mine? She'd slapped me! If that wasn't a wound, I didn't know what it was. But I didn't have the will, or the energy, to continue the fight. Some people thrive on high drama. I'm not one of them.

I rose and silently left the room. In the hall closet I found Gramps's old jacket. I wrapped myself up and hurried outside. The surprising midwinter thaw had ended and a blast of Arctic wind stung my cheeks. I lifted my face and gulped the icy air as if it were water in a desert. I walked very fast for about half an hour. It worked, as it always did. Still angry, but much calmer, I returned to the house and found my mother and Gram in the kitchen, cleaning up. "I'll help," I said from the doorway.

"It isn't necessary," my mother replied. "I'm leaving tomorrow. You'll have to help every night for two weeks."

"Gram?" I took a couple of steps toward her.

"Yes?"

"I would never hurt your head."

It wasn't much of an apology, but it was more or less accepted. She looked up from the pot she was scrubbing. "I'm sorry I slapped you," she said. Then she returned her attention to her work.

I went upstairs. In my room, I dialed Claudia's number. I let the phone ring and ring and ring, but this time no one answered at all. I hung up and then redialed, in case I'd made a mistake the first time. But I hadn't. There was still no answer.

Next I decided to try to reach Phil. I didn't know his phone number or even his mother's first name. I asked information if they had a number for a Doyle on Bartine Street. It was unlikely that there'd be more than one. There wasn't, but that fact didn't make any difference.

96

"I'm sorry," the operator said. "That is a nonpublished number."

"But this is an emergency," I begged. I was sure that if Phil knew I was trying to reach him, he'd want me to be able to.

"The party has requested a private listing." Though I knew I was speaking to a live operator, she sounded exactly like a computer. "We cannot divulge the number."

Foiled, I hung up. My family was furious with me. Geoff and I were through. Claudia had disappeared and I couldn't reach Phil. What wonderful event would happen next? Perhaps I'd fall down the stairs and break a leg.

I didn't know what to do now, except wait. Maybe eventually Phil or Claudia would show up in school.

EIGHT

The next day Claudia and Phil were still absent. After school I decided to walk over to Claudia's house. I couldn't walk to Phil's; it was too far away. Even from Claudia's I'd have a trek home. However, a hike of a couple of miles wouldn't do me any harm.

When I got there, I rang and I knocked. I knocked and I rang. I kept ringing and knocking, knocking and ringing, long after I was convinced that no one was home.

After twenty minutes, I left. I had a long way to go through a cold, leaden March afternoon. I walked with my chin tucked into the turtleneck of my sweater and my hands in my pockets.

Now I was really worried. What had happened to Claudia? She wasn't home with a runny nose or the flu. If she were, then she'd have answered the door. So where was she? In nineteenth-century novels girls who'd been involved in unsuitable romances were sent to Europe to forget their lovers. Could the Santoras have done something like that to Claudia? They might have shipped her off to a grandmother or an aunt someplace on the other side of the country. They might have enrolled her in a strict girls' boarding school where the cruel headmistress turned all the lights out every night at nine o'clock, fed the students gruel and wormy bread crusts, and allowed them to see their families only once a year, for two hours on Christmas Day. They might have incarcerated her in a lonely castle on top of a crag, surrounded by a deep moat full of crocodiles, with only a dwarf who'd had his ears and his tongue cut off to keep her company.

I entertained myself with similar lurid versions of Gothic novels and half-forgotten tales all the way home. My own house seemed as empty as Claudia's. The rooms were dim and silent. Mom was never home at this hour anyway, even when she wasn't on a jaunt to the other side of the world. Jonathan was in Hebrew school. As for Gram and Gramps, they could have been anyplace.

I was hanging my coat in the hall closet when the phone rang. I ran into the kitchen, snapped on the light, and picked up the receiver. "Hello," I said.

"Oh, it's you," Claire returned. "You're home. You weren't there a minute ago."

I took a deep breath. "I just walked in the door."

"Why weren't you on the bus?"

"I walked over to Claudia's house, and then I walked home."

"What did you do that for?"

"Well, you know, I've been worried about her. She hasn't been in school, and neither has Phil."

"So what happened?"

"She wasn't home, either. No one was."

"Probably both her parents work."

"But where is *she*? It's like she's disappeared off the face of the earth."

"Oh, come on, Dinah," Claire chided. "Just because you haven't seen her doesn't mean other people haven't seen her. Her mother and father probably know perfectly well where she is."

"Maybe I'll go back there tonight. You know, when they're likely to be home."

"They won't appreciate it," Claire warned.

99

"Look," I said, "if you just up and disappeared, wouldn't I want to find out what had happened to you?"

There was silence for a moment on the other end of the telephone. "Yes," she finally said, in a subdued voice. "But I'm your best friend."

Claire was jealous. She was jealous of Claudia. I tried to soothe her. "Claire, you'd look for me if I suddenly disappeared." I thought of a couple of our other friends. "But you'd look for Josie and Brenda, too. You know you would. A person doesn't have to be your best friend for you to be a little concerned about her."

"All right. But you're exaggerating this. I don't think Claudia has disappeared. Not actually."

But something had happened. I knew about things Claire didn't know about, like the Santoras' fury and Claudia's desperation.

I heard the door slam, and the sound of voices in the back hall. I turned to see my grandmother and Erna walking into the kitchen. Erna was carrying a box which she set down on the table. "Oh, Dinah," Erna exclaimed, "just wait till you see the dress I got for Jonathan's bar mitzvah. We bought it at Young Expressions." She rattled on, utterly ignoring the telephone receiver I was holding to my ear.

"Gram just came in," I said to Claire. "I'll speak to you later. If you have any thoughts about Claudia, call me." I hung up the phone and turned to the others. "What's going on here?" I asked.

"I needed a dress," Erna replied. "Mom didn't have time to take me shopping, so Gram did. Wasn't that nice of her?" I noted that "Gram." To Erna, my grandmother was no longer Mrs. Horowitz. Their intimacy had escalated.

Erna opened the box, pulled out the dress, and held it up under her chin. "It's lovely," I said, and I meant it. "Just get some off-white stockings and a pair of creamy patent leather pumps."

"You see?" Erna said, turning to Gram. "I knew Dinah would know what I should wear with it." She faced me again. "What do you think I ought to do with my hair?"

"Do you want the truth, Erna?"

She nodded slowly.

"Cut it all off."

"No!" she exclaimed.

"I knew you didn't want the truth." I grabbed her by the arm and pulled her out into the hall. Gram followed. I forced Erna to look into the mirror, while I stood behind her and pulled quantities of long, lank dark hair away from her face with one hand and brushed aside her bangs with the other. "See," I said.

The sight of her face unprotected by its accustomed covering seemed almost to frighten her. I knew she would have moved away from the mirror if I hadn't been holding on to her hair so tightly. But Gram said, "Dinah's right."

"You have a dainty face, Erna," I said. Then I added, to my own surprise, "Actually, quite a pretty little face. No need to hide it. Make an appointment with Kathy at Cut Ahead. She'll fix your hair up for you."

"Dinah's right," Gram repeated.

"Yes, I know," Erna said. "Dinah has perfect taste—"

"Oh, come off it," I interrupted.

"You do. It's just that . . . well, I'm used to my hair the way it is. I've always worn it this way."

I shrugged. "That's up to you, Erna."

"It's always scary to do something you haven't done before," Gram said. "I'll go to the hairdresser with you, if that'll make it any easier."

"You planning to adopt Erna?" I snapped.

Gram smiled. "Not officially."

"I wish you *could* adopt me," Erna said mournfully. "You understand me so much better than my own mother does."

We returned to the kitchen, where Gram heated up some water for tea. "I heard you talking to Claire as I came in," she said. "About finding Claudia. Is she lost?"

"I don't know." So far I hadn't told anyone at home about the reaction of Claudia's parents to the picture in the

Indian. Jonathan was so busy I hardly saw him, and it wasn't the kind of topic that came up when I was with him anyway. As for the others, I hadn't been on terms that inspire confidence with them for weeks now. But since Gram had asked, I told her exactly what had happened, as far as I knew.

"I could drive you over to Claudia's house after supper," Gram offered. "I could even drive you to Phil's house."

"Thanks," I said. "I'd appreciate that. I don't know what kind of welcome I'll get, but I feel as if I have to try."

"Does Geoff know about this?" Erna wondered.

"Geoff has nothing to do with it," I retorted.

"But he's Claudia's friend. He's been her friend for a long time," Erna said. "Longer than you."

"I know that." I whirled a spoon around in my cup so vigorously it produced a miniature tidal wave, causing the tea to splash over into the saucer and even onto the tablecloth.

"So maybe he knows what's happened," Erna offered mildly.

"Maybe he does," I admitted.

"So why don't you ask him?"

"Erna, don't be stupid. You know it's over between us."

"That means you can't even speak to him?"

"You have to help Claudia," Gram said, putting a plate of cookies down between Erna and me.

I slammed the table so hard with my fist that two macaroons landed on the floor. I was making as much a mess of this tea party as I had at the age of four. "I'm doing the best I can," I exclaimed. "It's your fault I can't do any more!"

Gram withdrew to the sink. "I'm sorry," she said. "I'm sorry I mentioned it."

Gram was full of sympathy for every teenaged waif in the state of New Jersey. Her own granddaughter was another story. But I wasn't going to say that. I wasn't going to go through what I'd experienced the night before. Instead, I rose from the table and headed out of the kitchen.

"Aren't you going to finish your tea?" Gram asked.

"Suddenly, I'm not very thirsty," I retorted sharply.

I left them and ran upstairs. In my room I turned the radio on very loud, sat down at my desk, and took out my sketch pad. I decided to draw the objects on my knickknack shelf. Doing that ought to take my mind off Geoff, my mind off Claudia, my mind off Gram, my mind off everything that was making me feel miserable.

It was a mistake because, of course, one of the objects on my knickknack shelf was the daffodil Smurf. I picked it up and held it for a moment suspended over the wastepaper basket. But I couldn't drop it. I just couldn't. I opened my bottom desk drawer and shoved it in a metal cookie box where I kept an old Girl Scout knife that no longer cut, half a dozen marbles, an eraser shaped like a unicorn, and a host of other rejected childhood treasures.

The knickknack shelf was safe now. I returned to my drawing. The ploy succeeded. In time, the work absorbed me completely. My mind was filled by each object in turn, as I concentrated on seeing it exactly and somehow transferring what I saw to the paper in front of me.

A shiver of surprise ran through me when the phone rang. I was so completely occupied by the drawings beneath my hand that there was no room in my head for the knowledge that phones could ring. The sound called me back to the world and shook the charcoal out of my fingers. I glanced at my watch. Six-fifteen. I'd been working for an hour and a half. Gram hadn't even called me to help get supper. Well, maybe Erna had been invited to stay and was giving her a hand.

My concentration had been broken, but I picked up the charcoal to begin again. Before I could draw another line, I heard Jonathan's voice outside my door. "Phone, Dinah," he called. "It's for you."

I lay the charcoal down and reached for the receiver. Claire, I thought. Maybe she was calling to say she'd had a flash of inspiration regarding Claudia. "Hello," I said.

"Hello. Dinah?"

His voice was unusually hesitant, but I had no difficulty recognizing it. "Geoff?"

"Yes."

He paused. I said nothing. I couldn't say anything. My heart was beating in my throat.

When he spoke again, his words rushed after one another, as if he thought he'd better explain himself as quickly as he could, before I scolded him or insulted him or hung up the phone. "I understand you're worried about Claudia. I'm worried about her, and about Phil, too. I just wanted to . . . well, talk to you about what we ought to do."

"How did you know I was worried about Claudia?"

"Your friend Erna called me. Just a little while ago."

"Erna?"

"Yes. She said you were over Claudia's house this afternoon and no one was home."

I was too amazed by what Erna had done to comment on it. I'd have to save that for later, after I'd digested it. "Listen, Geoff," I said, "Claudia hasn't been in school, either. Did you know that?"

"I hadn't really noticed," he returned. "But after Erna called, I thought about it and realized I haven't seen her around the last two days. I haven't seen Phil, either. I have history and gym with him, only he's absent quite a bit, so I didn't think too much of his not being there. But Claudia— she has to be at death's door to skip school."

"The fact that they're both absent—I think that may be significant," I suggested.

"I'm sure it is," Geoff agreed. "Listen. Can I come over? We can decide what to do."

I didn't hesitate. "Sure. Come on over."

"We're going to eat now. I'll be there right after. Seven-fifteen or so."

"Okay." He said good-bye and hung up. Slowly I replaced the receiver on the hook. I walked over to my bureau and stared at myself in the mirror. I lifted a tube of lip gloss from my makeup basket and applied it to my lips. I brushed some mascara on my lashes. I combed my hair. I decided the necklace I was wearing didn't look right with my sweater. I took them both off and put on others. Then, of course, I had to comb my hair again.

I knew I was acting silly. The fact that Geoff wanted to talk about Claudia didn't mean anything so far as he and I were concerned. And I didn't want it to. He had insulted my family and me. He hadn't even tried to understand us. So he and I were through. That was the way it was; that was the way it had to be.

But I couldn't help feeling glad that he was coming over. Did that mean I was a first-class jerk? Maybe—but you can't help how you feel. Well, perhaps you can, but it takes so much work that you better be sure it's worth it.

Downstairs, Erna was nowhere in sight and Jonathan was helping Gram get dinner. "Why didn't you call me?" I asked.

"Why didn't you come down?" Gram returned, without taking her eyes off the pot of stew on the stove.

"I was drawing. I was so absorbed I never even noticed the time."

Her voice softened. Gram could understand that kind of concentration. "I figured you were busy. I had Jonathan. He was enough today."

"I am enough," Jonathan sang in a falsetto voice. "I am enough," he repeated in a basso profundo. "I am enough, I am enough, I am enough."

"Which voice are you going to use when you chant your *haftarah*?" I asked. "Your soprano or your bass?"

"He's going to try for a nice easy tenor," Gram said. "Go ahead, Jonathan, call your grandfather. Tell him dinner's ready."

Jonathan left the kitchen and then Gram turned to me. "Geoff phoned you," she said.

"Yes, he did. He's coming over. It's only business."

"Business?"

"He wants to talk about what we can do, because he knows I'm also worried about Claudia."

"He figured that out?" She sounded amazed by evidence of such perception and sensitivity on his part.

"No," I admitted. "Erna told him."

"Erna!" She was as surprised as I had been.

"Erna called him."

"Imagine that."

"Yes, imagine."

Jonathan returned with Gramps, and the four of us sat down at the kitchen table for dinner. Geoff arrived while we were still eating the last of the berries Gram had frozen months before. On this day of surprises, Gram surprised me, too. She offered him a bowl of fruit. He accepted, sat down with us, and ate every drop. "Very good," he said. "Makes me think of summer."

Gram smiled. "I understand you're concerned about Claudia Santora."

He turned to her with a questioning glance.

"I know about her," Gram said. "Dinah told me."

Now it was me on whom he fixed his gaze. "It's all right," I said. "Gram understands a lot about unhappy kids." I knew that was a hard thing for him to believe, given her attitude toward him, but I also knew it was true, so long as the kid in question wasn't a relative. "She was going to drive me over to Claudia's tonight so I could see if her parents were home now. They wouldn't talk to me over the phone, but maybe they would in person."

"You don't have to, Mrs. Horowitz," Geoff said. "I'll drive Dinah. The Santoras have known me for a hundred years. They've got to talk to me."

"No, they don't," I reminded him. "They're really furious with you because you were in on the whole scam. The only person they're madder at is Phil."

"And Claudia," Geoff reminded me.

"You know," Gram said, "I just don't understand parents like the Santoras. They are beyond my comprehension."

As if our heads were all attached to the same string, Gramps, Jonathan, Geoff, and I all turned at once and stared at her. "You don't?" I asked in a quiet voice. "How come?"

"Don't they know that the best way to drive a teenaged girl right into the arms of the boy they disapprove of is to forbid her to see him?"

"It doesn't always work out that way," Geoff commented softly.

She looked at him for a moment, frowning. "No, no—you and Dinah, that's a different case."

"Is it?" Geoff asked. "I don't see how."

She didn't get angry. She seemed quite willing to explain. "No one in this house forbids Dinah—or Jonathan—to do anything. We've brought them up with a set of values which they've internalized, so we know that we can trust them to do the right thing. The Santoras may love Claudia, but they don't seem to respect or trust her. Phil may not be the young man they'd have picked out for their daughter, but they seem to have arrived at a negative judgment about him for some fairly superficial reasons—you know, a smart mouth, mother works in a diner, 'not like us,' that sort of thing."

"Like wrong religion," Geoff said, very softly.

"What?" Gram queried.

"You heard him," Gramps said with a sigh.

"You think my objections to you are as unreasonable as the Santoras' objections to Phil? Is that what you're saying, Geoff?"

"More unreasonable, maybe," Geoff said. His voice was louder now. "Phil does have some pretty tough characters for friends, and he is on probation."

"Oh," Gram said. "I didn't know about that." She eyed him sharply. "You, on the other hand, are perfect."

He had to laugh. "Sure," he said.

"Go ahead," Gram said. "Go on over to Claudia's house. Find out whose folks are reasonable and whose aren't."

Geoff stood up, and so did I. "Thanks again for the fruit," he said.

"Call me if you need me," Gram said. "I'll be here."

As he started the car, Geoff smiled. "She sure doesn't hesitate to tell you what's on her mind," he said.

"Gram, you mean?"

He nodded. "You know where you stand with her."

"I don't think you made her change her opinions," I said.

"I don't, either," he said. "But I suppose she really doesn't have anything against me personally, because if she did, she wouldn't hesitate to let me know."

"A privilege of age, she says. But so far as I can remember, she was always that way. Anyway, she isn't so awfully old—she's sixty-four. She could live to be ninety." I turned so that I could see his face. "You say what's on your mind, too."

"Not always," he replied. "But I did today."

I wondered why. Maybe it was because she'd offered him the fruit. Maybe that had broken the ice. And why had she done that? I didn't know. Perhaps certain habits of hospitality are more deeply ingrained than our firmest prejudices.

We pulled up in front of Claudia's house. The porch light was on and another light gleamed from a front window. Upstairs, all was dark. Together, we experienced a repeat of the scene I'd played earlier in the afternoon. We rang the bell, we beat on the door, and we rang the bell again.

"No one's home," I said. "They left a couple of lights on, but they're not home. That's to fool any thieves who might be looking for likely prospects."

"Yeah," Geoff said. "We leave lights on, too." We turned and started back to the car. "We'll try Phil's house now," he said. "Let's see what's going on there."

We arrived at Phil's in a few minutes. The broken main on Bartine Street had been repaired, so we didn't have to detour down by the river. We parked the car at the curb and walked up to the house. The lights were on here, too. We knocked. A moment later, a woman with lots of extremely blond hair piled on her head opened the door. She looked to be about the same age as Gram, who also bleached her hair, but to a somewhat less noticeable color.

"Hi, Mrs. Archibald," Geoff said. "Remember me? I'm Phil's friend. This is Dinah. She's a friend of Phil's, too. Is he here? We need to see him."

The question on her face disappeared, to be replaced by a worried frown. "No, he's not here," she said. "But please come in. I'd like to talk to you."

We entered the front room. The house was tiny and quite old, but bright with fresh paint, flowered slipcovers, pictures of flowers on the walls, and potted plants covering every available flat surface.

Mrs. Archibald didn't waste any time. "I'm so glad you stopped by," she said. "I haven't seen Phil for three days, and I'm worried sick. Do you know where he is?"

Geoff shook his head. "No. That's what we came to try to find out."

"No good," Mrs. Archibald said. "It's no good. I hope Claudia knows where he is. I can't imagine he'd go off without telling her. But he'd never forgive me if I called her house."

"No one's home at the Santoras'," I told her. "No one was there last night, either."

"I don't want to ask any of the neighborhood boys, and I can't call the police. For the same reason—in case he *is* in trouble." Her shoulders slumped, and in spite of the brightness of her hair and her clothes, she looked very tired. "He's been so good for so long. I thought he was through with all that stuff."

"Mrs. Archibald, I think he *is* through with all that stuff," Geoff said. "I think perhaps his disappearance has something to do with Claudia."

"Claudia?" Mrs. Archibald exclaimed. "But she's such a nice girl, such a good influence on Phil."

"The Santoras found out," I explained. "They found out Claudia was still seeing Phil, and they hit the ceiling."

Mrs. Archibald ran her fingers through her tight yellow curls. They bounced back into place as soon as she let go. "His mother went on a trip with her new boyfriend," she complained. "I don't even know the name of the hotel where they're staying. She was away when he stole that car, too. I'm always the one who has to deal with the things that go wrong."

I took up Geoff's litany. "We don't *know* that anything's wrong."

"When did you last see him?" Geoff asked.

"Sunday night. I don't see him mornings because I sleep late." She ticked the days off on her fingers. "Monday afternoon I went to work before he got home from the carpet store. And then on Tuesdays he works at the carpet store again. So I really didn't start to worry until last night when I got home from work and looked in his room and he wasn't there. But he could have been gone since early Monday."

"Anything go with him? Any clothes, money, anything like that?" I admired the questions Geoff was asking. He sounded like a TV detective.

"I'm not sure. I really don't know what he has and what he doesn't have. There's still stuff in his drawers. I can't tell if it's *all* his stuff. I don't know about money. I don't know how much he had. He didn't take any of mine, I can tell you that much."

"Did the school call, looking for him?" I asked. "If you're absent more than a day or two, the truant officer usually phones."

"If they did, they got no answer. Today I worked the day shift."

Geoff stood up and held out his hand. I took it, as easily as if I'd never stopped. He pulled me to my feet, and then kept my hand in his. "Well, Mrs. Archibald, try not to worry," he said. "We'll keep looking, and we'll let you know if we find anything out."

"Where are you going to look?" she asked.

"I have a few people I can talk to," Geoff replied. "I'll let you know whatever I discover."

She walked us to the door and let us out. "Good night," she called. "Thank you."

"Good night," I returned. And then, when we were

back in the car, I put my hand on Geoff's arm. "Where to next?" I asked.

He shook his head.

"You said you had a few people you could talk to."

"I just said that to make Mrs. Archibald feel better." He placed his hand on top of mine. "I don't know where to go next, Dinah. I don't know what to do. All I can say is that if he doesn't show up soon, she'd better call the police."

"I wonder if he is with Claudia," I said. "Because if he is, and she's disappeared, too, you can be sure that her folks already *have* called the police. And they've mentioned his name, for sure."

"Then the cops would have been here, asking Mrs. Archibald questions."

"So maybe they're not together."

"Maybe."

"But that's hard to believe."

"The Santoras," Geoff said. "We have to talk to the Santoras."

"Yes," I said. "Let's go back to their house. It looked like a place people planned to return to. We'll just go back there and wait."

NINE

We drove in silence, each of us occupied by our own thoughts. I don't know what Geoff was thinking about, but I was thinking about him. Not thinking about him, actually, so much as looking at him, at his features, sharply etched in the glow of a streetlamp, and then, as we moved out of the pool of light, once again shadowed and dim.

We had left behind the potholes, sagging fences, broken windows, and peeling paint of the east side. We were back in our part of Lenape, the section in which I lived, and Geoff and Claudia. Suddenly Geoff made a sharp right turn off Front Street, onto Winnetka Drive.

"This isn't the way to the Santoras' house," I said.

"I know," Geoff said. "I know the way to my own street."

"So where are we going?"

"Back to the east side." He swung the car to the right again and drove around the block.

"Why?"

"I think I know where they are. I want to see if I'm right. Then we can go to the Santoras—if we still want to."

"You think they never left Lenape?"

Another right, and then a left, and we were back on Front Street, traveling in the opposite direction.

"If they're together, which I think is likely. I was remembering the dance." His voice dropped so low I strained to hear it. "What a wonderful night."

"Yes, wonderful." My voice was no louder than his. "I don't know if Claudia and Phil think it was so wonderful."

"It was bound to come out," Geoff said, "sooner or later. They couldn't keep a secret like that forever. And they can't keep this one, either."

"Which secret, Geoff? Where are they?"

"The night of the dance, remember, Bartine Street was closed—a water-main leak or something."

"Yes, I remember. We had to detour picking Phil up."

"And taking him home. Twice we passed an abandoned apartment house, with all the windows boarded up."

"Yes—the one Phil's father used to live in."

"Phil said his father owned it, with some other guys."

Now I understood. "You think Phil and Claudia are there."

Geoff nodded. "Claudia talked a lot about homeless kids in big cities who move into abandoned buildings."

"But, Geoff, it's so cold!" I exclaimed. The entire East Coast was still in the grip of the cold snap that had descended upon us along with the month of March. The papers ran pictures of Florida farmers warming orange trees with smudge pots. I shivered, imagining Phil and Claudia huddled together under a blanket in a bleak, unheated room.

"Phil's handy," Geoff said. "Maybe he could work something out. Anyway, let's go see."

He found the house on River Street without any difficulty. It was utterly dark. Not the barest light glimmered through a crack in a single one of its boarded windows. Streetlamps provided the only illumination of the empty road. Occasionally, a car passed, but I felt as if it were a windup toy, operating without a driver. Human beings no longer inhabited River Street, at least not at night.

113

"No one's here," I said.

"Let's make sure." Geoff removed a flashlight from the glove compartment and climbed out of the car. I followed. A sign had been fastened to the front door. "For Sale or Lease. Reichert Realty."

Geoff turned the knob, pressing his shoulder against the door, but it didn't give way. "It's locked," he said. "Probably bolted, too." He stepped back and gazed upward to the top of the building's four stories, which was as high as a structure in Lenape went, with the possible exception of a couple of office buildings downtown. "I could knock and shout, but if they're all the way on the top, they wouldn't even hear me, and someone else might. If they are here, I really don't want to give them away."

"If they are here, they can't stay," I said. "They have to come out eventually. But I don't think they're here."

Geoff, however, hadn't given up hope. "Well, I *will* make some noise if I have to," he said. "Only let's go around to the back first."

He snapped on his flashlight and took my hand. We made our way through a narrow alley paved in cracked cement and littered with beer bottles, old newspapers, and soggy cardboard cartons. The small yard in the rear of the building, surrounded by a rusted mesh fence, was full of the same sort of garbage. It was much darker here than on the street, dark and cold.

A screech cut through the night. I jumped. "What was that?" I cried.

Geoff put his arm around me and pulled me close. "Just a cat."

"I don't like it here," I announced.

"It isn't exactly the Garden of Eden," he agreed. But he made no move to depart. "Look!" he said. "Look up there."

I followed his pointing finger and noticed on the third floor a faint, flickering gleam. The boards had been removed from that window, and a thread of light, like a candle flame, showed against the blackness.

We approached the back door. Geoff played the beam

of the flashlight over its surface. The plate around the lock was marked with scratches, as if someone had been working on it with a screwdriver. Again, Geoff put his shoulder against the door and turned the knob.

"This one isn't locked," he said. "I think the lock's been picked. But there's something against the door, blocking it." He tried again. His quarterback's shoulders were wide and strong. The door itself moved a little, but he couldn't budge whatever it was that was in the way. Frustrated, he backed off. "I have to get up there," he muttered.

"Maybe it's just as well if you don't," I suggested. "We don't know for sure that light is Phil and Claudia's. Maybe it belongs to some drug addicts or criminals or something."

"All right, I'm going to call," Geoff decided. "Back here, no one should hear me, except whoever it is that's in the house. And if it turns out to be someone we're not too anxious to meet, we'll run like hell." He squeezed my fingers. "Okay, Dinah?"

"Okay, Geoff."

He stood aside, lifted his head, and cupped his hands around his mouth. "Phil," he called. "Phil. Claudia. Claudia." He didn't raise his voice to its greatest volume. He didn't actually shout. But anyone near a third-floor window should have had no difficulty hearing his clear, carrying tone. "Claudia," he repeated. "Phil. Phil. Clau-dee-aaa."

"Maybe they don't recognize your voice," I suggested.

"It's Geoff," he called. "Your friend, Geoff."

A head appeared at the window. In the dark, I couldn't see who it was. But then a voice called, "Geoff? Are you alone?" and I knew it was Phil. His tone was much softer than Geoff's. He spoke just loud enough to be heard from that distance.

"Dinah's with me," Geoff replied. "No one else."

"I'm coming down," Phil said. "I'll let you in."

We waited by the door for a few moments. We heard footsteps, and then the sound of a heavy piece of furniture being pushed aside. The door creaked on its hinges and there stood Phil, like Geoff, carrying a flashlight, and staring at us with wide, unsmiling eyes. "So you found us," he said.

"Sooner or later someone had to," Geoff said.

"Yeah, I guess so. Better you than Mr. Santora. Come on up."

We entered what appeared to be some sort of utility room or service porch. Phil shut the door. "Help me," he said to Geoff. "We have to push this old sofa back against the door."

"Is that really necessary?" Geoff asked. "You'll just have to move it again to let us out. No one else is coming. No one else knows you're here."

The two flashlights made the room a place of invisible corners and shadowy, unidentifiable shapes. But I could see Phil nod his head. He turned and headed toward the front of the building. We followed him through a door, into a hallway, and up some stairs. "Watch your step," he said. "The linoleum is coming up. You could trip on it."

The smell of damp rot and layers of dust made me cough. I fastened the neck snap of my down jacket and then shoved my hands in my pockets. It was bitterly cold in that place, colder than it was outdoors, as cold as a tomb.

In the second-floor hall, boards creaked. I thought I heard the scuttering of rats. I grabbed Geoff's hand and held it as tight as I could. We climbed another flight of stairs. Now we were on the third floor. Phil pushed open a door and we entered a room lit by a candle flickering in a glass holder on the floor. Though it certainly wasn't warm in the room, it was noticeably less cold than the hallways and stairs. There was no furniture. Along one wall lay an open suitcase and a cardboard box, both piled with clothes.

Claudia stood near the candle. "Welcome," she said. "Welcome to our humble abode. Come into the kitchen. It's warmer there. Almost normal."

The kitchen contained a rickety card table, two mismatched chairs, and two sleeping bags. It was much brighter than the other room; several candles burned in cups and

116

glasses surrounding a brave red geranium in a pot in the middle of the table. And Claudia was right—it was much warmer, about the temperature Gramps kept our house during the night. The four burners of the stove were lit, and so was the oven. I could see the broiler flames through the open door.

"Phil and I will sit on the sleeping bags," Claudia said. "You two take the chairs." We obeyed. "You see," she exclaimed, almost gleefully, "all the comforts of home. We were lucky. We found the table and chairs in other apartments. And for some reason, in this apartment, the gas had never been turned off. If it weren't for that, we couldn't stay here. There's an outside faucet that wasn't shut off, either, so we can even carry up water."

"How do you flush the toilet?" I wondered.

"Oh, we have a bucket," Claudia said. "Phil was smart enough to bring that along. He said you never know when a bucket will come in handy. He brought rope, too, and electric wire, and some tools."

"You're regular survivalists," Geoff commented dryly.

"Your grandmother's worried about you, Phil," I said. "She's worried sick. She seems like a nice lady."

"Tomorrow I'll go out and call her," Phil said. "I'll tell her I'm all right."

"Your parents must be kind of worried, too," Geoff suggested, turning to Claudia.

"I guess they are." The lift of her chin and the narrow line of her mouth made it clear that she thought they were getting what they deserved.

"But, Claudia," I exclaimed, "you can't just stay here. You can't just stay here forever."

"Well, of course not," she returned. "We know that. We'll leave once we've worked out what to do next."

"What are you living on?"

Claudia rose from the sleeping bag and opened a cabinet over the sink. She took Phil's flashlight and shone it inside. I could see some cans and boxes arranged on shelves. "We came here and explored this place. When we realized we could manage here for a while, we pooled all our money. We used most of it for a few utensils and some food, and we bought everything all at once, first thing."

"We don't want to leave here too often, and certainly not during the day," Phil said. "Someone we know might see us."

They were like two little kids playing an elaborate game of house, adding a few forbidden twists to bring the excitement up to a level they certainly hadn't experienced as six-year-olds.

"But what are you going to do next?" Geoff asked quietly. "When the food and the money run out? I mean what have you decided?"

"We're exploring all sorts of possibilities," Claudia replied. She glanced at Phil, and then returned her attention to the cabinet, carefully closing the doors. "I'd like to offer you something, but we have to conserve."

"Listen." Phil stood up, too. "At first I thought it was terrible you'd found us, but now maybe I think it's a good thing. I've got to get a car, I've just got to. Claudia won't let me steal one—"

"That's the surest way to be found," she retorted with a touch of her old acerbity. "You know that as well as I do, Phil."

I was glad to hear her say that. It showed she hadn't entirely lost touch with reality.

"All right, all right," he said. "Can you help me get one, Geoff? What do you say?"

Geoff turned and faced him. "What are you doing, Phil? Asking me for my car?"

"Just a lend, Geoff. Until we get somewhere we can find work and a place to live. Somewhere no one will find us."

Geoff rose from his chair and sat down on the sleeping bag next to Phil. He didn't say, "How would you ever get the car back to me?" He didn't say, "How will I explain to my parents that the car they bought for me has somehow disappeared?" He just looked at Phil and spoke very quietly. "You're dreaming. There's no such place."

"All those photos of missing kids on milk cartons," Claudia said. "No one's found them."

"Is that really what you want for your families and friends?" I asked. "The kind of terror those parents are experiencing?"

Claudia moved toward Phil. He put his arm around her and pulled her to him, so that the curve of her body fit perfectly against his. There was no space between them.

"They're not going to separate us," Claudia insisted. "They're not. We love each other. They think just because we're young, our love can't be real. They think we'll get over it. Well, we don't want to get over it."

"I guess they think it's real enough," I said. "Otherwise they wouldn't be so upset by it."

Claudia's eyes widened. Apparently it was the first time she'd thought of that.

"There is a place you can go," Geoff said. "For a while, anyway, until you work things out."

"Where's that?" Phil sounded as if he didn't believe him.

"The JINS shelter."

"That's for juvenile delinquents. We're not delinquents. We haven't done anything wrong." You could have cut Phil's defensiveness with a knife.

"Most of the kids at the shelter haven't done anything wrong, either," I explained. "Nothing worse than run away, maybe, like you."

Phil and Claudia were silent.

Geoff hurried to take advantage of their hesitation. "You should talk to Dinah's grandmother. She volunteers at the shelter, and she can explain it all to you. She seems to really understand kids."

Other people's kids, I amended mentally. But I nodded vigorous agreement. I thought the best thing they could do was talk to Gram.

"I knew when I saw you that it was over," Phil said.

"Does that mean you'll come with us to Dinah's house?" Geoff asked.

Phil looked at Claudia. Claudia looked at Phil. He leaned down and kissed her, a gentle, lingering kiss. For a moment it was as if we weren't even there. Then Claudia said, "I guess Dinah's grandmother is better than my mother and father."

"Or the police," Phil added.

Persuading Phil and Claudia to leave their hideout hadn't proved terribly difficult. I suppose deep down they had known they were just playing house. They had known they weren't ready for the real thing. We helped them gather their stuff together and load it all into the trunk of Geoff's car. There wasn't much; it took only one trip.

We drove to my house. The way it was ending surprised me. There were a million things I wanted to say to Geoff, things like "What was the exact moment at which you turned into such a big fan of Gram's?" But I couldn't say any of them in front of Claudia and Phil, so I kept my mouth shut.

"Dinah, you go in first," Geoff said. "Kind of prepare your grandmother."

"What's the matter?" Phil snapped. "I thought you said we could trust her."

I hopped out of the car. "That's what I'm going to make absolutely sure of," I said.

Phil scowled. Claudia laid her head on his shoulder and shut her eyes. They weren't happy, but it was too late to do anything about it now.

In the house, I found my grandparents in the family room, doing, as usual, four things at once. "Where's Geoff?" Gram asked, looking up.

"Listen, Gram." I was standing right by her chair, looking down at her. "If two kids had a problem they wanted to talk over with you, would you run and tell their parents all about it first thing?"

She pushed her needle back and forth through the material and allowed it to remain there. "You're talking about Phil and Claudia."

I nodded.

"Their parents have to know where they are," Gram said softly. "They must be told."

"I know that," I said. "But would you listen to them first? Maybe they could stay in the JINS shelter for a while, or at least maybe Claudia could, until her parents calm down."

"It's possible," Gram said.

"Are they here?" Gramps asked.

I didn't reply.

"We'll listen first," Gram said. "We promise that. We won't do anything until we've listened. Right, Lou?"

Gramps nodded.

"Gramps," I said, "would you mind awfully not being here? I didn't say anything about you, and they're kind of nervous. We had trouble enough convincing them they could trust Gram."

Gramps gathered up his newspapers and books and went upstairs. I don't think he was terribly unhappy about leaving. My distaste for life as soap opera I'd perhaps inherited from him. Gram, on the other hand, thrived on crisis. She was addicted to excitement.

I went out to the car. "It's okay," I said. "Come on in."

"She won't call anyone?" Phil asked.

"She'll listen to you first," I said. "Then you'll decide together what to do." Of course, she would insist that their families be informed of their whereabouts. If they wouldn't do it themselves, she would do it, I knew. But she'd promised to listen first, so I felt I didn't need to go into that. Maybe I was betraying Phil and Claudia, but I didn't think so. To have abandoned them in that empty building—that would have been a betrayal.

In the bright light of our family room, Phil and Claudia looked tired and gray. They sat next to each other on the sofa, perched on the edge like nervous birds, clutching each other's hands as tightly as a drowning man grasps a lifesaver. "We love each other, Mrs. Horowitz," Phil said.

"We won't let them separate us," Claudia added.

Gram let them talk. Occasionally she asked a question,

but mostly she just listened. Her eyes were fastened on their faces. It was clear that she was taking in every word they said. I wondered if any grown-up had ever listened to them so hard. I wondered if things would have been different for them if some grown-up had. They leaned back on the sofa. Their hands broke apart and they gestured as they spoke. They seemed to melt beneath the warmth of her regard.

Then she told them about the JINS shelter. She said she thought Phil should go home. "There's no reason for you not to," she said. "Your folks aren't giving you any trouble. Claudia should go to the shelter." She explained that most residents were referred by the court. "But I have influence," she said with a little smile. "I think they'll take you in if I ask them to. And then, from there, you can call your parents."

"I don't want to call my parents," Claudia insisted.

"The social worker will be there when you meet with them," Gram assured her. "It'll make a big difference, having a third party present."

"We want to be on our own," Claudia said. "We want to be together."

Now Gram took Claudia's hand. "You have to think of this. Your parents may have called the police already. I can't believe they haven't."

"Well, I suppose by now they have," Claudia admitted. "But they didn't do it right away."

"Why not?" I asked.

"I left them a note. I said I was leaving on a five o'clock train out of New York for Uncle Joe's in Pittsburgh. They didn't find the note until they got home from work last night. I picked Uncle Joe and Pittsburgh and a train instead of a plane so they'd figure it would take me all night to get there. Which means it wasn't until today that they'd have called Uncle Joe and found out I wasn't there. Which means it wasn't until today that they'd have called the cops."

"Very clever," Gram commented, almost without expression. She was doing well with them because she was keeping any judgments about them to herself. She wasn't even letting them color her voice or her facial expressions. She could do that when she wanted to do it, which was never with me or Mom or Jonathan. "However," she continued, "it's only a matter of time before they track you down. The police may be at Phil's house already. Isn't it better for you to tell them where you are yourself, than to be dragged back there, kicking and screaming? Think about Phil," she added softly. "Think of the trouble he'll be in if it's the police who find you."

"They can't do anything to Phil," she cried. "This was my idea. I persuaded *him*."

"That's what you should tell them," Gram said. "In a room with a social worker present, to keep things calm."

Phil and Claudia were up against a wall. But Gram left them some room to hope. They knew they had to do as she suggested. They also knew she didn't think they were just a couple of stupid kids. In the end, they agreed to part for a while—Phil to return home, Claudia to go to the JINS house.

Gram went into the kitchen and phoned the shelter. "They said you could come on over right away," Gram explained, as she returned to the family room. "I'll drive you."

"I'll keep you company," I announced.

"Geoff," Gram said, "you take Phil home."

"I can hear Nana now." Phil sighed as he put a hand over an ear. "I'll be deaf for a week. When I was little and I did something wrong, she'd go after me with a dish towel, an eggbeater, a trowel—whatever was in her hand."

"Did she get you?" Gram asked.

He laughed. "Not usually. I got bigger, and she gave up trying. The hitting, not the yelling. She'll never give that up."

"Good," Gram said. I wasn't exactly sure what she meant by that, and I didn't ask.

Gram, Geoff, and I went outside to move Claudia's stuff into Gram's car. Phil and Claudia hung back a little, to say good-bye. Geoff placed Claudia's suitcase in Gram's trunk. "I'd like to come back," he said. "After I drop Phil off, I'd like to come back. I want to find out what happened at the shelter."

"It's late," Gram said, slamming the trunk door shut. "You can call."

"Gram!" I exclaimed. "He's coming back. I want him to come back."

Geoff looked at me and smiled a little. Then he turned to Gram. "I'm coming back."

"Oh!" She waved her hand at him. "Come back, come back. What do I care? Come back."

Hand in hand, Phil and Claudia walked out of the house. Phil climbed into Geoff's car, Claudia into Gram's. Phil leaned out the window. "Call me," he shouted.

"They have phones there, Mrs. Horowitz?" Claudia asked.

"Yes, Claudia. It's not a prison. A prison is one thing it definitely isn't."

"That'll be an improvement." She waved her hand out of the window. "Good-bye, honey." She sounded almost jaunty. "Don't worry, I'll call. I'll call right away."

TEN

When Gram and I arrived back at the house, we found Geoff sitting in the kitchen with Gramps, drinking cocoa. Cocoa with marshmallows was Gramps's single culinary accomplishment. "The secret," he said, "is whipping it with a wire whisk. That's what *some* people are too lazy to do." By *some* people, he meant Gram.

Geoff took a sip. "I guess it is the best cocoa I ever had." Maybe also the only cocoa since he'd reached puberty.

Gram sat down at the kitchen table. "Do you have enough for us?" she asked.

Gramps filled two more mugs, and we sipped the thick, sweet stuff while Gram reported on what had happened at the JINS shelter. "I spoke to Mr. and Mrs. Santora first," she explained, "and then I put Claudia on. They're coming down in the morning. I'm delighted that Phyllis Trimbach will be working then. Of all the social workers on the staff, she's the most competent."

"Gram had some job persuading them not to rush over there tonight," I said.

Nodding, Gram popped an Oreo into her mouth. "No wonder I'm starved. It took a lot of energy to talk them out of descending on Claudia immediately and swooping her away. After all, we have no court order remanding her into our temporary custody."

"So how did you talk them out of it?" Geoff asked.

"By sort of implying that we did have a court order," Gram admitted. "And mentioning over and over again how terribly late it was, and how the house parents were in their night clothes, and the kids were mostly asleep."

"Oh, boy," I murmured, "I sure hope it all works out. If Mr. and Mrs. Santora still won't let Claudia see Phil, she'll run away from them again. And next time she won't be persuaded back so easily."

"Had they called the cops?" Geoff asked.

"They had," I said. "But not until late in the day."

"Yet they must have known she wasn't at her uncle's early this morning. What made them wait so long?" Geoff wondered.

"Well, you see, they didn't want anyone thinking Claudia was a bad girl," I explained. "They didn't want that idea to get around. So they spent the day looking for her themselves. They went to Phil's house, but of course no one was there, and they didn't know where Mrs. Archibald works. They went to the school, but I guess they were so circumspect about what questions they asked that no one there was alarmed. And then, after school, they went to a couple of her girlfriends, again being very careful about what they said, which was silly, since her friends knew perfectly well there was trouble in Claudia's house. Between one thing and another, I guess they didn't get to the cops until maybe four or four-thirty this afternoon."

Geoff shook his head in amazement. "Suppose she wasn't with someone who cared about her the way Phil does? She could have been in terrible trouble. She could have gotten hurt or something."

"They're foolish people," Gram announced. The Santoras weren't present, so she had no need to be sparing in her judgment. "Their values are all screwed up. They've behaved like a pair of thick-headed bulls."

"You know, Mrs. Horowitz, you ought to let me come

to Jonathan's bar mitzvah." Geoff's tone was perfectly matter-of-fact. "Look at me. I'm not a bull. I don't have horns."

I understood the connection between her remark and his. I'm sure she did, too.

"Neither do I," she snapped.

"Yes," Geoff replied. "I know that."

"I like you, Geoff." Her tone was milder now. "I like you a lot. That's all the more reason for not inviting you to the bar mitzvah."

Geoff looked bewildered. I must have, too.

Gramps put his mug down on the table. "You'd better explain that to them, Miriam."

"You know what I mean, Lou."

"I think so." Gramps pointed at Geoff and me. "They don't."

Gram consumed another Oreo before she spoke. I guess this time she needed to think a bit before she put her feelings into words. Now that she knew Geoff, she really did like him and she really did want him to understand.

"Geoff," she said, "if you were stupid or mean or insensitive, there'd be no chance that Dinah would be your girlfriend. She might go out with you a few times because you were attractive and popular and your interest flattered her, but it would never last if she discovered you weren't a decent person. I know and trust Dinah well enough to say that." She turned to me. "Am I right, Dinah?"

I nodded. "And vice versa, too."

"Naturally," Gram said. "If Geoff found out you were horrible, he'd drop you like a hot potato. Well, we know you're wonderful, Dinah, and now we know Geoff's wonderful. So you like each other, you get involved, you stay involved. Why should you give each other up? There aren't so many wonderful people walking around on the face of this earth that you can afford to do that." She paused and looked at Geoff.

Geoff watched her intently, not saying a word.

"All right," Gram continued. "So then one day, there we all are, Gramps and me and Dinah's mom and Jonathan and your parents, down at City Hall, standing in front of a magistrate, watching you two get married." Now she fixed her attention on me. "No rabbi, Dinah. No chanting of the seven blessings. No breaking of the glass as all the guests shout '*mazel tov*.' And no children brought up to know about and care about and carry on the Jewish tradition." The gaze she fastened on me was like a rope. "And if not *your* children, Dinah, then whose?"

"Gram, sometimes if a Jew and a non-Jew marry, the kids are raised Jewish anyway. We both know families like that, right in our own synagogue." I reached for a name and fortunately hit upon one. "Like the Mytelkas."

"It isn't easy," Gram intoned in the voice of doom.

"But it's possible."

"It's more likely to go the other way."

"Hey, wait a minute," Geoff interrupted. "I haven't proposed marriage to Dinah. I haven't even thought of it."

"You probably never will," Gramps said. "But it could happen. You have to admit, it could happen."

Geoff was silent. I reached out and put my hand on Gram's. "Gram, being Jewish might be the most important thing in the world to you." It was *an* important thing, but it wasn't *the* important thing. If it were, we wouldn't be living the way we did. But this wasn't the moment to accuse her again of hypocrisy. Anyway, I'd learned something. My folks weren't any more hypocritical than I was. We were all ambivalent. We all wanted it all ways at once.

I took a deep breath. "Being Jewish is important to me, too, but so is Geoff. I'm not talking ten years down the road, I'm talking now. I'm not talking wedding, I'm talking bar mitzvah. I want Geoff to be there."

"Still," Gram said.

"Yes. When Mom gets back, I'm asking her again." I rose quickly to my feet and glanced at the clock above the kitchen sink. "It's after midnight. Tomorrow's school."

Geoff stood up, too. "Thanks for the cocoa."

"I'll see you to the door."

In the hall, he put his hand on my shoulder. "Do you forgive me?" he asked.

"Yes," I said. "Do you forgive me?"

He nodded. "I'll try not to be so sensitive."

"I'll try not to be so hot-tempered."

"I'll try to be more understanding."

"Me, too."

He leaned over and brushed my lips with his. And then, suddenly, his arm tightened around me. He gave me a real kiss, a long, hard one, and inside of me I felt the lump that had been sitting in the bottom of my stomach for the last week melt like a dirty snowball. He released me with a sigh. "Dinah," he said, "let's not mess it up again."

"No matter what my mother says when she comes home?"

"No matter what she says."

He left then. I called good night to Gram and Gramps, still talking at the kitchen table, and climbed upstairs. It was then, for the first time in hours, that I thought of Erna. Of all the unbelievable things that had marked the evening, she was perhaps the most unbelievable of all. She had phoned Geoff. I couldn't imagine why, but I knew I owed her something. Actually, I owed her a whole lot.

In the morning, when I sat down next to her on the bus, she turned and stared at me. "Aren't you saving a seat for Claire?" she asked.

"I'll talk to Claire later," I said. "Right now, I want to talk to you. Why did you call Geoff yesterday?"

She blanched and her whole body tensed. "Oh, Dinah, I'm sorry. I'm so sorry. I thought I was doing a good thing. I thought I was doing you a favor."

"It's all right, Erna. You did do me a favor."

She relaxed with a sigh. "Oh, good. You and he are on again."

"Yes, we are." The next words weren't easy to say, but I made myself say them. I wasn't going to be more stubborn than Gram. Hers was stubbornness enough for one family. "I want to thank you, Erna, for calling him. It was a nice thing to do, and it worked. Even if it hadn't worked, it couldn't have done any harm."

She nodded. "That's what I thought. You had broken up anyway. I couldn't make things worse. I mean, I think of you like a sister. I had to do something."

"What did you tell him?"

"I said you needed him. You needed his help."

I lifted my hand and touched her hair. "Listen, you don't have to cut off this mop. Come over the night before the bar mitzvah and I'll do it for you. I'll fix it so it stays off your face. And then you can decide if you want to go ahead and have it cut—you know, sometime later."

"Should I wash it first?"

"I'll wash it and blow-dry it," I said.

She grinned. I'd never seen such a broad smile on her face. "Gee, Dinah, thanks."

"You're welcome, Erna."

I opened my history book and began reading. Enough, after all, was enough. She was busy, too. She took a compact and comb out of her purse and spent the rest of the ride combing her hair.

The day after she returned from Australia, my mother, Gram, and I drove over to Clover Lake Country Club. Mom and Gram were checking the menu and room arrangements for Jonathan's bar mitzvah reception for the last time. "You come, too," Gram had said. "Your mother's practically color-blind. If we leave it up to her, the flowers will clash with the table linen."

"Yes," Mom said, "come along. We need your opinion."

Between the two of them, they were perfectly competent to decide a matter as trivial as the color of the napkins. But I went.

The three of us sat side by side on gilt chairs in the office, waiting for the catering manager. "We have to put the Kasselbaums at your table," Mom said.

"Over my dead body," Gram retorted. The two of

130

them had renewed their arguments about the seating arrangements almost the second my mother got off the airplane.

"You told me I had to invite her."

"You did have to invite her. But I don't have to sit with her. It's bad enough listening to my friends rattle on about their grandchildren. I draw the line at Yorkshire terriers."

I rested my arm on the back of my mother's chair. "I still want Geoff to come to the bar mitzvah." I said. "I still think you should invite him." Mom knew all about the night we'd found Phil and Claudia in the abandoned apartment house. She also knew Geoff and I were on again. She'd heard the outline over the phone when she'd called from Sydney and I'd filled in the details as soon as she'd arrived home.

"Over my dead body," Gram repeated.

"I wish you'd try to avoid that particular cliché," my mother suggested.

"You think someone might take me up on it?" Gram asked. "Who, I wonder?"

"Well . . ." Mom turned and looked at me. "I *am* inviting Geoff to the bar mitzvah."

"You are? Oh, Mom!" I leaned forward and kissed her.

"But, Ellen, we agreed," Gram protested. "The three of us agreed. You, me, and your father. We agreed."

"I don't like what's going on between the Santoras and Claudia," Mom said.

"Of course not," Gram returned promptly. "Neither do I. It's awful. But what has it got to do with Geoff and the bar mitzvah?"

Claudia had returned home. The Santoras remained adamantly against her relationship with Phil. She saw him only at school. I was sure they were thinking of running away again, but neither of them said a word about that or much else to anyone. I had the feeling they were planning their next move very quietly and very carefully. They weren't going to rush into anything this time. Meanwhile, Gram was really working on the Santoras. She was trying to get

131

them to accept the idea of counseling. Claudia was all for it, Mrs. Santora was beginning to think it wasn't such a bad idea, and Mr. Santora was dead set against it. I hoped he relented before it was too late.

"Has Mr. Santora succeeded in breaking up Claudia's romance?" Mom asked mildly.

"Of course not," Gram said again.

"Quite the contrary. He may have actually driven Phil and Claudia closer together."

Gram nodded. "Very likely."

"I'm not going to be a Mr. Santora," Mom said. "And neither are you."

"How dare you suggest there's the slightest resemblance between me and Mr. Santora!"

My mother didn't rise to that bait, but instead turned to me. "It's too late to mail an invitation. When Geoff stops by tonight to pick you up, I'll hand it to him. A new postal service. Personal delivery."

I squeezed her shoulder. "Thanks, Mom."

Gram sighed. "You're making a big mistake. But you're her mother."

"Yes," Mom agreed. "That's true."

"Why don't you hand Mr. Chickering an invitation, too?" I suggested.

Mom's eyes widened. She pressed her lips together and shook her head. I didn't broach the subject again.

Ms. Pickwick, the catering manager, strode through the office door, a rainbow array of linen spread out on her arm. "You wanted burgundy napkins, didn't you, Mrs. Adler? Burgundy napkins with white tablecloths?"

"We'll get to that later," my mother said. "That's the least of it. First, I'd like to look at the room again. I want to make sure the tables are arranged to leave enough room for the Israeli dancing. And there has to be a good spot where my father can make the blessing over the bread."

Mom, Gram, and Ms. Pickwick left the room. I trailed behind, dreaming. Someday it would be my wedding we were arranging. Would we have the reception here? Would the ceremony take place under a canopy, would we dance the hora, and would the bride and groom be lifted up in chairs and paraded around the room? There was so much to being Jewish, so much more than religion, such a web of custom, habit, attitude. What would happen if I had a son? Would he have a bar mitzvah? I'd want him to. I knew that much, anyway.

When Geoff came to get me, I led him into the family room. An envelope with his name on it lay on the table. Mom picked it up and handed it to him. "For you."

Geoff smiled. "I accept," he said, without even opening it.

"Good," Mom returned. "We look forward to having you with us."

"How about you, Mrs. Horowitz?" He took a step in Gram's direction. He wasn't afraid of her any longer.

She didn't look up from her embroidery. "I'll behave myself," she said.

"They're having a sale at Herman's," Geoff announced. "I'm going to make Jonathan a tennis goody bag. Balls and head bands and wrist bands and sneaker laces and a book about tennis and all good stuff like that. I'll wrap each thing individually and put it in a big box and wrap the box, too. It'll keep him busy for days."

"He'll love it," I said.

"I'm giving Dinah a present," Gram said.

"You are?" I knelt beside her. "That's super. What's the occasion?"

"Jonathan's bar mitzvah, naturally."

"There's nothing like a present when you don't deserve one. They're the best kind."

"I'm giving Jonathan a present, of course," Gram replied. "But I'm giving you one, too."

"What is it?"

She lifted a corner of the tablecloth spread out on her lap. "This," she said. "It's almost done."

"Oh, Gram. Oh, Gram." I put my arms around her

and hugged her. "Your masterpiece. Thank you, thank you. It's the most wonderful present anyone ever gave me. I'll treasure it always and forever."

She looked into my eyes. "Use it, Dinah. Don't let it rot in a chest. Put it on your table for holiday dinners. If it gets a few wine stains on it, so what? Pretty things are meant to be used."

I moved my palm over the blue-green vase. "I will."

She stretched the top edge of the material between her two hands. "I'm working on the border. The same color as the vase. Little six-pointed stars, all the way around the edge."

David's star. There was no more clearly identifiable symbol of Judaism than the Magen David. Even non-Jews knew what it meant. Even Geoff. I was perfectly aware of what Gram intended by this gift, but I accepted it anyway. We could talk about it some other time. "That'll be lovely," I replied quietly. "Thank you, Gram."

"You're welcome." Her voice dropped to a whisper. No one else in the room could hear what she said. "I love you, Dinah."

"I love you, too, Gram."

We'd all had high expectations for Jonathan. He surpassed them, chanting his biblical portion and long sections of the service in a fine, clear voice that reached to the furthest corner of the sanctuary. His speech would have made a statue cry, but he carried it off without a catch in his throat. He talked about how sorry he was not to have known his father, but how proud he was sure his father would have been if he could have seen the wonderful way in which his mother, grandmother, grandfather, and even— even—his sister Dinah had brought him up.

We were all dabbing at our eyes with tissues when the rabbi called us to join Jonathan for one of the best prayers in the whole Jewish liturgy, the prayer recited on special occasions. Jonathan, Mom, Gram, Gramps, and I stood in front of a huge room packed full of the people we loved, gazing out at them, holding hands and smiling through our tears, as we recited the familiar words. "Blessed art Thou, O Lord our God, King of the Universe, who has blessed us, and sustained us, and kept us in life so that we could celebrate this joyful season."

It had been a long service, two and a half hours. And the service was the least of it. There was so much else besides. I sat next to Geoff, wondering what he was thinking. I could explain it all to him, but it would take me weeks. Years maybe. Would he even want me to? I didn't know if he cared.

And how much did I care whether or not he cared?

Later, after the hugs and kisses among all the relatives, and the cocktails and the dinner and the noisy games the bandleader persuaded Jonathan and his friends to play, Geoff and I danced. We wrapped our arms around each other and moved as one, silently, dreamily, while the music enveloped us like a golden cloud. I won't care either, I told myself. Not now. I would permit nothing to matter except the moment I was in.

His lips were next to my ear. "This is nice," he whispered. "This is just so nice."

"Yes," I replied. "So nice. The nicest thing."

Choices. Living was choosing. Over and over again, each day, each hour.

For the moment I'd made my choice.

Just for the moment.

ABOUT
THE
AUTHOR

BARBARA COHEN is a graduate of Barnard College, where she earned membership in Phi Beta Kappa, and has also received an M.A. degree from Rutgers University. Mrs. Cohen has lived in New Jersey all of her life, but has traveled extensively in the United States and abroad. She is the recipient of the Association of Jewish Libraries' Sydney Taylor Body-of-Work Award, and has received many other prizes. Among her popular books for young adults are *Roses* and *Lovers' Games*. She and her husband live in Bridgewater, New Jersey, and have three grown daughters.